★

Buzz had been going strong all evening: drinking, dancing, talking and drinking some more. Now he stood up and raised his glass. "To all of us," he shouted. "May we all be lucky in life and lucky in love!"

Buzz brought his glass down and took another sip. As he did, the glass slid out of his hand and crashed to the floor. He leaned his head forward and stared at the splinters.

He let out a long groan. Then his body crumpled, and he fell, face down to the floor.

Melanie reached the collapsed man first. He was breathing, although his breaths were shallow. His eyes were closed, his face ashen. The other guests and waiters thronged around, hands over their mouths in concern or shaking their heads in bewilderment.

"I'm so glad Amy and Paul left earlier," Fonnie muttered to herself. "What a terrible way for a wedding reception to end."

★

*Previously published Worldwide Mystery titles by*
*HELEN GOODMAN*

THE BLUE GOOSE IS DEAD
TOXIC WASTE
MURDER IN EDEN

HELEN GOODMAN

WORLDWIDE®

TORONTO • NEW YORK • LONDON
AMSTERDAM • PARIS • SYDNEY • HAMBURG
STOCKHOLM • ATHENS • TOKYO • MILAN
MADRID • WARSAW • BUDAPEST • AUCKLAND

*Dedicated to my new sons,*
*Bill Warren and Rusty Kiley.*

**MURDER AND MISDEEDS**

A Worldwide Mystery/January 2009

First published by Alabaster Books.

ISBN-13: 978-0-373-26661-6
ISBN-10: 0-373-26661-8



**Printed in U.S.A.**

# Acknowledgments

Many thanks to the members of my critique groups: Dixie, Larry, Dave, Lynette, John, Emogene, Joanne, Nancy, Betty, Dorothy, and Diane. Your comments are invaluable.

Special thanks to Patty for proofreading these pages.

*O world...*
*confused and filled with*
*murder and misdeeds.*
—Thomas Kyd (1594)

# ONE

Fonnie Beachum smiled tenderly as she reread the invitation. Of course, she'd known the contents before receiving it, but it was good to see it in print. She rubbed her soft hands over the soft-textured vellum, traced the embossed names, *Amy Beachum Hendley* and *Paul Augustus Trent.* What a lovely couple they were. Both in their late forties, both survivors. Amy was divorced and Paul was a widower. Fonnie was thrilled her daughter was being given another chance at happiness. She nodded in approval at the upcoming date. February fourteenth. When better to have a wedding than on Valentine's Day?

She glanced up at her grandson, his lanky legs sprawled out under the kitchen table, his blond hair still mussed from sleep. "Beacon Hill Beach," she said reading the location, "at the Shepherd by the Sea Chapel. Isn't that a marvelous name? Like there's a special blessing hovering over the chapel."

"There is," Brian said, "but only for sailors and fishermen. I don't know how Mom got it in her head to get married there. It would have been a lot simpler if she'd just come back here to Groverton and gotten married in our own church."

"Simpler for us, but not for their friends in Virginia.

I think they made a wise decision to have the wedding midway between her home and ours. That way no one has more than a few hours to travel and we can all enjoy the North Carolina beach." Fonnie added another spoonful of sugar to her already sweetened coffee, took a sip. "I've never been to Beacon Hill Beach but Amy says it's lovely—small, not too commercialized yet. And it's a plus that Paul's law partner owns a motel there. I don't remember his name. Do you?"

"Edgar Myers. Seems like an odd investment for a lawyer to me."

"Anyway, Amy says it's close to the chapel and he's giving all the wedding guests reduced rates. Mighty nice of him."

Fonnie slowly slathered grape jelly on her piece of toast. "I wish we could stay a few days after the wedding. It's been nearly two years since I've been to the beach, since the summer before my stroke. Now I'm back on my feet, I'd love to walk the sands, commune with the seagulls. The wedding is on a Thursday. It'd be nice to stay for the weekend. Do you think you could get some time off work?"

Brian shook his head as he gulped his third cup of breakfast coffee. "No way. You know the police force is short handed since so many of the national guardsmen have been called up. Besides, February isn't exactly the best beach month. They could have waited a while. Mom's acting like a giggling teenager going on her first date."

"Love will do that to you. You'll find that out one of these days." Fonnie beamed at Brian. "I just hope I'm still around when it happens."

"In that case, I hope you're planning on living to be a hundred because it won't happen any time soon. I'm enjoying the bachelor life too well. Which reminds me—I've got a date tonight. Won't be home for supper."

"That's good because I won't be cooking."

Brian pushed back his chair, got up and stretched his six foot plus frame. His blue uniform emphasized his bulging biceps, his rugged torso. He's so handsome, Fonnie thought, no wonder his little black book is full. But, she smiled in pride, he's more than just good looking. He's sweet and kind and a mighty good cop.

"And why aren't you cooking?" He turned back as he headed out the door. "You got a date, too?"

"As a matter of fact, I do. A shopping date. Keisha is coming by. We're doing lunch, then looking for my mother-of-the-bride dress. After all that, I'll be too tired to cook supper." Fonnie finished her toast and looked back at Brian. "Any suggestions?"

"You mean about the dress?"

Fonnie nodded.

"Not about the dress." Brian hesitated. "But maybe you should do something about your hair."

Fonnie's hands flew up to her head, patted the frizzy reddish-orange curls. "You don't like the copper-kettle color?"

"You mean, the Brillo-pad look? Yeah, I like it. But you might tone it down for the wedding."

Fonnie scowled. "Did your mother put you up to this?"

"No. Not at all. I think she rather enjoys telling her big-city pals that her mother is an escaped circus performer." He snatched his cap from the coat hook and gave her a wink. "But wouldn't it be fun to surprise her with a new, sophisticated, aristocratic do?"

Fonnie wadded up her napkin and aimed for his head. "You better get out of here or I'll give you a new do."

Brain laughed. "Tell Keisha 'hey' for me. Maybe you could get her to go to the wedding and spend a few days with you at the beach. She must be a glutton for punishment if she's taking you shopping."

The door slammed behind him before Fonnie could come up with a retort. But as she sipped the last of her coffee, the idea that Brian had tossed out as a joke began to take root. Maybe Keisha would go with her.

"LET ME GET THIS STRAIGHT," Keisha said, stirring her iced tea so vigorously that it splashed onto the table, "you want me to go to the wedding, then stay on and walk the beach with you for a few days?"

Fonnie nodded. "That's right. And I'll pay all the expenses. Sound good?"

"And what exactly am I to be?" Keisha gave Fonnie a teasing smile. "Your companion? Your black maid? Your pooper-scooper-upper?"

"All of the above, but mostly just a friend." She stared across the table at the young girl with the beautiful bronze-colored skin. "I don't need a baby sitter, but it would be nice to have a friend along."

"It's rather a new idea, though." Keisha took a quick gulp of tea and set the glass down carefully. "It's silly I know. But until last month I was your home-health aide. Sometimes I forget you're not my boss anymore."

"I never was your boss. You're the one who did all the bossing. You insisted I do my exercises. Forced me to walk without my cane. Kept telling me I could do my own housework." She squeezed Keisha's hand. "You were right. I did need to regain my independence. And thanks to you, I did." Fonnie sat up straighter and squared her shoulders. "And I could probably walk the beach alone, too. But I'm just a little nervous about it. You know I still tire easily. And besides, it'd be more fun with a friend."

"Indeed it would. And I think I can cut a few classes without a problem. I'll go with you if you promise one thing."

"And that would be?"

"That you stay out of trouble."

"What trouble could I get into when we'll be staying practically next door to the Shepherd by the Sea Chapel?"

# TWO

AMY WAS WAITING for them in the Beachside Motel lobby. Even dressed in a causal blue pant suit, she looked every bit the successful business woman that she was. If she had any wedding jitters, they didn't show. Keisha stepped to one side as the bride-to-be rushed out and grabbed her mother around the waist. "Make the trip all right?"

"Well, we're here, but let me tell you, for a college kid, Keisha doesn't have much smarts when it comes to reading road maps. We got messed up trying to bypass Raleigh, got on some cow path that had neither gas stations nor McDonalds, missed our turn-off and had to back-track five miles. I sure wouldn't want to ride to New York with her."

"You needn't worry about that," Keisha said. "If we ever go to New York together, we're gonna fly and you can bitch to the pilot all the way."

Amy laughed. "Mom, you ought to be ashamed—giving Keisha such a hard time." She hugged Fonnie again. "You look great. But what have you done to your hair?"

"What about my hair?" Fonnie caressed the soft waves, as shiny and silvery as a new quarter. "You don't like it?"

"I love it. You look so…."

"Sophisticated and aristocratic?"

"Actually, I was going to say prim and proper, but aristocratic fits better."

"You'd better say that. I've never in my life been accused of being prim and proper. Actually, the hair was Brian's idea. He thought I would have a better chance of snagging a boyfriend if I didn't look so much like a dance-hall floozy."

"He may be right. And speaking of Brian, where is that handsome son of mine?"

"He'll be along shortly. He probably had to stop and eat a couple of times. He thinks he's still a growing boy."

Keisha opened the trunk of the car and got out their luggage. Amy picked up one of the bags and steered Fonnie toward the door. "Come on. There's some people I want you to meet and Paul is anxious to see you. You too, Keisha. There's someone special I want you to meet."

"Sounds good. I'll just move the car and be right in."

KEISHA NEARLY SALIVATED at the someone special that Amy was leading towards her. He must have climbed right out of the pages of *Ebony,* she thought, or maybe he's a brother to that gorgeous black detective on her favorite TV show.

"Stephon Weber. Keisha Riggs." Amy acted like she was presenting a piece of candy to a hungry child. But Keisha wasn't sure if she was supposed to be the hungry child or the piece of candy. It didn't matter. What she had imagined might be a boring event suddenly looked more promising. She extended her hand and it was quickly swallowed up by his bigger one.

"Stephon is the latest addition to our real estate agency," Amy said. "He's already making a big splash in the market."

"How nice." Keisha smiled as she slowly reclaimed her hand. "I'm pleased to meet you." Unable to think of anything else, she added. "Looks like we'll have lovely weather for the wedding."

"Yes. Lovely for this time of year. Amy tells me you're in college."

"Yes, she's a business major," Amy said before Keisha had a chance to answer. "And Mom told me she made the dean's list in her first semester." Amy looked up as the front door opened. "Got to go and do my greeting duties. You kids get acquainted now and I'll catch you later."

Stephon laughed. "Do you get the impression we're being thrown together for the duration of the festivities?"

"Looks like, but Fonnie may not like the idea. She'll expect me to be around whenever she wants me. If I'm not, she won't be too happy. And if Fonnie's not happy, ain't nobody happy."

"I'm looking forward to meeting her. Amy has told me a little about her mother, her remarkable recovery after her stroke, and her forays into crime fighting. Sounds like an interesting person. But right now I'd like to learn more about you."

Yes indeed, Keisha thought, this little foray is definitely looking up. Imagine, a man who isn't all about "me." She grinned at him. "And what would you like to know?"

"In the first place you don't look like a college freshman. Is this a career change for you?"

"That's a kind way of putting it. Actually, I had to work a few years to scrounge up some money. I was a nurse assistant in a nursing home. That's where I met Fonnie. She urged me to go on to school and become an RN. But nursing isn't really my bag, so I decided to go into Business Administration."

Keisha looked around the room and saw Fonnie sitting with Paul and some other guests. "It looks like Fonnie is in good hands so she won't be looking for me any time soon." She turned her attention back to Stephon. "I don't know a soul here except the bride and groom. Do you?"

"Yes, I've met Paul's partners and some of his friends. That's Buzz Garrison, one of his partners, talking to Fonnie now."

"The one that's leaning against the counter and holding his stomach as if he were in labor?"

"That's the one. He must not be feeling well. He and his wife, Midge, arrived before lunch about the same time I did, and he looked then like he was nursing a hangover."

Keisha studied the man. Probably in his fifties, tall, well-built, but with the beginning of what was generally known as a beer-belly. "Poor fella. He should be in bed."

Stephon nodded. "It looks like he's telling Fonnie his problems."

"Better her than me. Who's the other guy with Paul?"

"That's our host, Edgar Myers. He's the senior partner in the law firm. I heard he's planning on retiring soon and he bought this motel as an investment and a retirement home. But I hear his wife isn't too happy with the plan."

"Sounds like a winning idea to me. Isn't he young,

though, to be retiring? He looks like he's only in his mid-fifties. He must have done well."

A smartly dressed, thirtyish blonde came up to Edgar, wrapped her arms around his shoulders and whispered something in his ear.

"Wow," Keisha said, "if that's his wife he certainly has done well because that suit she's wearing didn't come from any store I shop in."

"That's Lula. I think the term for her in the business world is 'trophy wife'."

"Quite a trophy. She's lovely."

"Yes, she is. But from what I've heard, Edgar has to work hard to keep her happy."

Stephon's gaze went from Edgar to where Buzz and Fonnie sat. He motioned to Keisha. "Looks like Fonnie is trying hard to get your attention."

Keisha looked quickly over to her traveling companion. "Uh-oh. I'd love to talk more, but I think I'd better get Fonnie to her room. She needs to rest a bit before the rehearsal and dinner."

"Sure. I'll see you later."

"THANK GOODNESS you rescued me from that Garrison fellow." Fonnie kicked off her shoes and stretched out on her bed. "I don't care if he is Paul's law partner, he's a total bore. Kept talking about how bad he felt, stomach cramps, nauseated, dizzy. Asked me what I thought he had. Some people think just because I used to be a nurse, I can diagnose, treat, and cure everything from hangnails to hangovers."

"Can't you? I've always thought you were pretty smart."

"Of course I'm smart. I told him it sounded like he got the flu bug and he needed to stay in bed for a couple of days. And he certainly didn't need to spread it around."

Keisha nodded her head. "And what did he say to that?"

"Said he hadn't been around anyone with the flu, and he wouldn't miss being an usher for Paul's wedding for anything."

Keisha walked over to the window and pulled up the blinds. "Well, forget about him. We'll just try to avoid being around him." She gazed out of the window. "You have a superb view of the beach. It's beautiful but the water looks angry."

"Angry? What do you mean?"

Keisha shrugged. "I don't know. Like the water gods are upset. They think we don't respect their power. I think that's why the sailors built the chapel, to appease a jealous Neptune."

Fonnie waved Keisha to the door. "Get out of here, youngun. You're giving me the shivers. Next thing I know, you'll be telling me Neptune has put a curse on me."

Keisha shuddered. "Or on me."

# THREE

LIKE SOME OTHER GUESTS, Brian arrived while Fonnie was taking her nap. The wedding party was small, but a few people decided to come up early to avoid driving on the day of the ceremony. When Fonnie came back to the lobby, Paul was greeting everyone and insisting they attend the dinner after the rehearsal. Fonnie and Keisha were introduced to Amy's friends and business associates, to Paul's daughter, Clara, and her husband, Tony Cauthen.

Clara was nearly a duplicate of her father. She had thick dark hair, high cheek bones, and deep green eyes. Fonnie dubbed them Irish eyes.

Tony was a redhead with an engaging smile and a boisterous laugh. He laughed as he shook Fonnie's hand. "I was just telling Paul he'd better enjoy tonight. It's the last night before his life sentence."

Fonnie gave Tony a decidedly frosty stare. "Is that your definition of marriage, young man?"

Before Tony could say anything else, Clara stepped between them. "Don't pay any attention to him. He's just trying to be funny." She held out her hand to Fonnie. "I'm delighted to meet you, Mrs. Beachum. Amy has told me a lot about you. She's so proud of the progress you've made after your stroke. And I know you must be proud of her also."

"Proud as a peacock—raising a son alone and at the same time making a name for herself in the business world. Your daddy is a lucky man if I do say so myself."

Clara laughed. "That's what he keeps saying. And I'm lucky to get her for a step-mom. I'm sure they're going to be very happy."

Tony slipped his arm around Clara's waist. "Yeah, I was just kidding earlier. Maybe they'll have as much happiness as we have. Huh, Honey?"

Fonnie thought she detected a slight edge to Clara's voice as she answered, "Ours would be hard to match, Tony."

Paul came up to Fonnie and took her by the arm. "Hate to pull you away, but you've got to meet my Uncle Jeremiah. He's going to be my best man, and he's been eyeing you ever since you walked into the room."

Fonnie's step quickened as they neared the stately gentleman. He was tall, broad shouldered, had a full head of gray hair, and a billboard smile. She reached out her hand and he grasped it in both of his. "So this is the lovely mother of the bride. I've got a feeling we're going to become good friends."

Fonnie replied with a formal, "Glad to meet you." Inwardly she echoed his words. Yes, she thought, very good friends. After a brief chat with Jeremiah, Paul hauled her off to meet the rest of the wedding party.

At the end of the introductions, Fonnie's head was swimming with names and faces which she kept trying to connect. The one name she had no problem remembering was Buzz Garrison, the usher who looked like a leftover from a keg party.

Fonnie went so far as to warn Paul that he ought to

insist on Buzz sitting out the rehearsal and the following dinner. "That man is a walking germ. He'll end up infecting everyone here."

"I talked to him," Paul said, "but he insists he doesn't have a fever. Thinks he just ate something that disagreed with him. He and Midge drove up from Florida. He started feeling bad before they left. I'm sure he's not contagious. Don't worry. I'll keep an eye on him. If he's not better soon, I'll get him to a doctor."

AFTER THE REHEARSAL, Amy and Paul led the way back to the motel, where the rehearsal dinner would take place in a private dining room. The chapel was only a half-block from the motel so most people walked. However, Fonnie noticed that Midge Garrison had driven their Lexus over and Buzz, who had tried his best to keep a smile on his face, crawled into the passenger seat and dropped his head down on his chest. Fonnie shook her head. "Stubborn fool," she muttered to herself.

When Keisha came up to walk with her to the motel, Fonnie demurred. "You go ahead. I think I'll go back inside and sit a bit, take in the ambiance of this lovely chapel. I love old buildings, especially churches. They often speak to our souls when we take time to listen."

Keisha frowned. "Are you sure?"

"I'm sure. I can walk back by myself when I'm ready." Fonnie glanced down the steps where a very tall, very dark, and very handsome man leaned against the railing. "I think Stephon is waiting for you. Run along now."

When the chapel was empty, Fonnie leaned her head

back on the pew, took a deep breath, closed her eyes. She liked the smell, a little musty from seldom used hymn books combined with the lemon scent of recently dusted pews. Tomorrow there would be the added fragrance of the wedding flowers and the lit candles.

A sense of serenity settled over her. Yes, the Shepherd was here, calming the angry sea, watching over those who were about to take a long journey, by water, by matrimony, or simply by growing older. Her own journey had already been a long one, but Fonnie felt there was much more to come, and she was eager to see what lay ahead. It'd been quite a while since she'd felt this way. She breathed a heartfelt 'Thank you' to the Shepherd by the Sea for restoring her sense of hope and expectation.

She'd been fascinated by the life-size statue that stood on the front steps of the chapel, welcoming all who entered. The brick church and the statue both faced the ocean while a narrow sidewalk led from the street that ran behind the church to the front. The shepherd's arms were outstretched to calm the waves, to calm the worshiper's fears. The corners of his eyes and mouth both crinkled upward, a message of reassurance and peace.

Fonnie opened her eyes and studied the inside of the small sanctuary. It was plain—almost stark, but the dark wood was smooth, mellowed from the touch of petitioners through the years. She could picture the sailors, their wives and sweethearts, praying for safe passage. Her eyes went to the candles on either side of the altar, and she said a silent prayer for the two souls who would be united the next day.

A noise in the back of the chapel startled her and she jerked her head around. A shadow loomed before her. Footsteps sounded in the quiet. Fonnie rose to her feet, her heart raced, a chill went through her body. Her voice wavered. "Who are you?"

The shadow stopped. A soft voice answered her. "I'm sorry. I thought everyone had left. Just came to lock up." He walked closer, smiled at her, stuck his hand out. "I'm the caretaker. Didn't mean to disturb you."

Fonnie reached out and shook his hand. "I'm the mother of tomorrow's bride. I was just sitting here and thinking."

"Aye. Weddings tend to do that. They make a person stop and think. I can come back later if you want."

"No. No, I'm ready to go." Fonnie scooted out of the pew and started toward the door. The caretaker followed behind her. Fonnie paused and looked around again. "It's a beautiful little church. Do you know its history?"

"That I do. It was built in 1884. This was a fishing village then. The year before, several local men were lost at sea in different storms and hurricanes. Some of the God-fearing widow women started the idea that they needed a church dedicated to those who went to sea. A church to bless them as they went out, where the women could come to pray for their safe return."

"What a lovely idea. It must have been hard for a woman to sit and wait for her man to return."

"My grandmother said during the First World War, she remembered coming here to pray for her father who was fighting in France. She said it didn't matter what port the men sailed out of, they knew our own Shepherd by the Sea was looking after them."

"How inspirational. What denomination is it? It didn't say on the sign in front."

"Non-denominational. Had regular services until after the Second World War. Now it's a tourist attraction, used only for special occasions. I'm going to lock up tonight because you have things ready for the wedding. But otherwise, it's left open so tourists can come in at any time."

"How nice. And you've never had a problem with vandalism?"

"Never a problem from land or sea. Several hurricanes have tried to blow it away, but the Shepherd has always protected it."

"That's marvelous. And I can feel His protection all around me." Reluctant to leave the peaceful chapel, Fonnie again looked toward the dais. It was elevated higher than in other churches she'd been in. If there had been a preacher in the pulpit she would have had to bend her head back slightly to see his face. "I guess the pulpit is built high to force people to look heavenward."

He nodded in agreement. "That and to make space for the hidden room underneath."

Fonnie jerked her head around. "Hidden room?"

"Yes. It was built to be used as a shelter during hurricanes. There's a trap door under the lectern with stairs that leads down to a fair-size room. It could probably hold twenty people if they huddled together. They even added lights and a bathroom when the church was modernized. But it's not used these days. Most people have enough sense to evacuate when a big one's heading this way. And then there's the armory, further inland, for large emergencies."

"A hurricane shelter in a basement? What about the danger of flooding?"

"The builders thought about that. The chapel's foundation is actually in a sand bunker. The only exposed part is a small area that fronts on the street. The only way it could flood is if the entire town flooded."

"How interesting," Fonnie said. "Well, I guess I'd better be going. I've taken up too much of your time already."

"No problem. I enjoy talking about the Shepherd and His church. And you can be sure He'll be smiling on the wedding party tomorrow."

# FOUR

FONNIE GOT BACK to the motel just as some of the guests were heading for the dining room. Brian came up and gave her a squeeze. "I was about to send out a search party. I knew you'd never deliberately miss a free meal."

"I've been communing with the past, soaking up some peace for my soul. Wouldn't hurt you to do some meditating while you're here."

"I might do that while Melanie and I are strolling in the moonlight tonight."

"Who's Melanie?"

"Melanie Peacock. I just met her a little while ago. She's the niece of Paul's friends, the Peacocks. You met them this afternoon—Hank and Doris."

"Oh, yes. I remember them. A delightful couple. But I don't remember meeting Melanie."

"She rode up from Miami with them. The Peacocks and the Garrisons were enjoying a winter break in the sunshine state. Melanie's a nurse at Miami General. She dropped in to visit her uncle and aunt, learned they were coming up here for a wedding and decided to ride along."

"Just like that? She invited herself to the wedding? Does she even know Paul or Amy?"

"She does now. You'll like her, Gram. She's quite a gal."

"Sounds like. In my day, nurses couldn't get off work at the drop of their caps to go gallivanting around." Fonnie gave Brian a warning look. "And don't you dare say something about things have changed since the Dark Ages."

"I wasn't going to say that at all. It just happened that she had some time off coming and things were slow at the hospital." Brian took Fonnie by the elbow and led her into the dining room. "Come on. I want you to meet her."

Fonnie allowed herself to be dragged over to a slip of a girl standing by a ficus plant. She had on a pale pink gauzy dress, a charm bracelet that jangled when she moved and a large sterling silver ring on her left hand. Her blonde hair was swept up, but several tendrils were allowed to cascade causally down her forehead and over her ears, giving her a look of careless perfection. She had a dazzling smile and smelled of magnolias.

Fonnie had planned on disliking the girl who had barged in uninvited, but two minutes after their introduction, Melanie had charmed her way into the older woman's heart.

"I can see where Brian gets his good looks," Melanie said, "his firm chin, his determined eyes. I know you must have been a terrific nurse. You seem like such a caring person."

Fonnie blinked a couple of times. She wasn't accustomed to flowery compliments. She could fling insults with the best of people, but these accolades left her speechless. She finally managed a soft, "Thank you. I'm sure you're a very good nurse, also. So perceptive."

Their mutual admiration society was interrupted by Jeremiah. "I think the best man ought to have the choice of dinner partners, and Fonnie, I would be honored to have your company."

"And I'd be delighted," Fonnie said. She waved a tiny goodbye to Melanie and Brian and smiled at Jeremiah as he took her elbow and led her toward a table. Since this was a motel dining room, there was no head table, and guests sat wherever they wished.

Jeremiah and Fonnie were nearly to their destination when he momentarily dropped her arm to move a chair out of the way. A red-coated waiter, bearing a tray of filled iced tea glasses, emerged from behind a potted palm. The waiter, apparently intent on reaching the far side of the room, looked straight ahead, while at the same time, Fonnie glanced at her reflection on the mirrored wall. Neither noticed the other.

Their collision was not a pretty sight.

KEISHA RESCUED FONNIE in the midst of the waiter's profuse apologies. She whisked the drenched woman off to her room to change clothes. Jeremiah waved after her, "Hurry back. We've got a lot to talk about."

They did hurry. Keisha gave Fonnie little chance to moan about her ruined dress. "No time for that now. We're not going to let a little mishap spoil the evening. We both have handsome gentlemen waiting for us."

"You're right," Fonnie said. "Got to keep the big picture in mind." She yanked some black nylon pants and a red sweater out of the closet. "These will have to do. My scintillating conversation will more than make up for any lack of formal dress."

In fifteen minutes Fonnie was ready. Keisha pushed her out the door. "You go ahead. I'm going to put your dress to soak in cold water. It may take out some of the tea stains. I'll be down shortly."

Keisha finished her task, then went to her own room to touch up her hair and makeup. As she came out into the hall again, the door across the hall opened. The woman exiting the room turned around and shut the door very quietly while Keisha pulled her door shut with a bang.

The other woman jumped. "Oh, you startled me. I thought everyone was downstairs.

"Not quite," Keisha said. She decided she didn't owe Midge Garrison an explanation, but she was curious about the woman's husband. "I hope Buzz is feeling better."

Midge smiled. "Yes. Yes, he is. Thank you for asking. But he decided he'd rest tonight so he would feel up for the wedding tomorrow. He said he didn't want anything to eat." They started down the hall toward the elevator. "I still think it's a flu bug."

Midge shoved the elevator button twice with her index finger. Keisha got the impression that here was a woman who hated to be kept waiting, who liked and expected to be in control. The elevator must have picked up her vibes because it responded immediately. Midge shoved the "close door" button almost before Keisha was all the way in. "I told Buzz time and again he needed to take the flu vaccine, but no, not smarty-pants Garrison. He said last year the vaccine made him sick and he wasn't going to take that chance this year." Midge's voice rose as the elevator descended. "Well, you can see where that got him. Sick as a dog and making me miserable—waiting on him, listening to him whining. I'll be so glad when this wedding is over. If he's not better then, I'm going to dump him in a hospital and leave him there." She tossed her head and stalked out of the elevator.

Keisha watched her disappear into the dining room. Another example of wedded bliss, she thought. She hoped Amy and Paul would escape the tentacles of a marriage gone sour. Keisha had seen so many bad ones, she was beginning to think the chances of happily ever after were as remote as winning a lottery. She enjoyed men, liked dating, but getting married was not part of her long-term plan.

When she entered the dining room, Stephon smiled and waved to her from across the room. He stood up, pulled out her chair, touched her hand. Yes, she thought again, she really did enjoy being around men.

She glanced over at Fonnie and Jeremiah. They also seemed to be enjoying themselves. For a moment Keisha wished she could eavesdrop on them. Just what, she wondered, did Fonnie mean by "scintillating" conversation?

AFTER ASSURING JEREMIAH no harm had been done in the mishap, Fonnie began their chat with a question. "Are you the uncle with the pet armadillo?"

Jeremiah squinted, adjusted his glasses, peered at Fonnie. "I must have missed something. What does an armadillo have to do with anything?"

Fonnie grinned. "I'm just trying to get Paul's family straightened out in my head. Amy mentioned an eccentric uncle to me when she first started dating Paul. She said he had a pet armadillo and collected ping-pong balls." Fonnie took a sip of tea. "Of course, she's been known to elaborate on the truth at times. But I thought I'd better check it out."

"She was right about one thing," Jeremiah said. He took his time slathering butter on his baked potato, cut a piece of steak, and waited for Fonnie's response.

"All right, already. Tell me. It's the ping-pong balls?"

Jeremiah shook his head. "It's the eccentric part. It runs in the family. But I fear Paul may have missed that gene. He seems too normal to be a Trent. Dreadful shame, but we can't all be blessed."

Fonnie dropped her fork, sat back and crossed her arms. "I knew I was going to like you. I bet you even believe in unicorns."

"What's not to believe? I rode one over a cliff when I was nine. Broke my arm, but it was a small price to pay for the ride."

A choking sound escaped from behind Fonnie's napkin as she tried to control her laughter. "And what do you do for fun these days?"

"I've got to admit I've slowed down some lately. I still play hop-scotch with the neighborhood kids and ride my ATV in the woods behind my house, but I've given up rock climbing and parachuting. It just wasn't much fun after Agnes died. She was my long-suffering wife, passed on seven years ago. When she wasn't around to tell me how crazy I was, it kind of punctured my balloon. Know what I mean?"

Fonnie nodded. "I think so. Half the fun of being eccentric is watching normal people react to your foolishness."

"Right. But I haven't given up the Polar Bear Club yet."

"Okay, I'll bite," Fonnie said. "And what do you do in the Polar Bear Club?"

"Swim."

"There's nothing eccentric about that. I used to love to swim. I may even get back to it. The YMCA in our town has a new pool."

"You didn't let me finish. We swim—in the ocean—in the wintertime—in below freezing temperatures."

"Ouch! That's not eccentric. That's downright crazy."

Jeremiah threw back his shoulders, took a deep breath. "It's what I owe my good health to. It builds up the immune system. I haven't had a cold in years. I have the heart and lungs of a man thirty years younger. If you ever need rescuing just call on me."

"I'll do that."

"I was beginning to think you might need rescuing after the rehearsal. I waited for you outside the chapel to walk with you. When you didn't appear, I went back in and saw you chatting with some other man, so I left."

"That other man was the caretaker. He was telling me the history of the chapel. It was most interesting, especially the part about the secret room."

"You mean the hurricane room? That's no secret. There's an article about it in the Chamber of Commerce newsletter that's placed all around town and in every motel room."

"Oh, I guess I hadn't gotten around to reading it yet. Anyway, I enjoyed listening to him." Fonnie sipped her coffee, then gave Jeremiah a full-face smile. "But not as much as I enjoy listening to you."

# FIVE

THE WEDDING WAS LOVELY. Buzz, only slightly green, was the perfect usher when he guided Fonnie to her seat. Dressed in an oyster-gray wool suit and with her hair carefully coiffed, Fonnie was pleased with her appearance, especially when Keisha whispered, "You're as pretty as an angel."

The real angel, though, was the bride. Amy, beautiful in her off-white chiffon dress, carried a bouquet of blue forget-me-nots. Brian stood tall and proud as he escorted his mother down the aisle. Her only attendant, Clara, in a simple A-line blue dress, gazed at her new stepmother with a look of admiration. Paul wore a smile that bounced off the walls. Jeremiah handled the duties of best man without a hitch.

Odd, Fonnie thought, how life's most wondrous events were over in a matter of moments. Months of anticipation and years of wonderful memories afterwards encapsulated in a few fleeting minutes. She sighed as Amy and Paul exited the little chapel. "Thank you, kind Shepherd by the Sea," she said under her breath, "for the perfect ceremony. Now extend your protection over them as they start this new journey."

THE PERFECTION OF the wedding carried over to the reception. When it came time for Amy to throw the bridal bouquet, Fonnie tried to push Keisha to the forefront, but a young cousin of Paul's made the catch. The party went on as people drank toasts, munched on decadent pastries, danced, laughed, joked. Amy and Paul danced with each other until Amy was snatched away by other men and Paul made the rounds of all the women.

At one point Paul stopped the band long enough to thank everyone for coming. Then waving their tickets to Bermuda, the happy couple slipped out. Their departure left barely a dent in the festivities. Fonnie knew they had instructed Edgar to keep the party going as long as anyone wanted to stay. Ostensibly, it was a BYOB affair since the motel didn't have a liquor license, but the bar was well stocked.

Most everyone danced, but Keisha and Stephon stole the show. No matter what kind of music the band was playing, Stephon managed to add some frenetic steps that left Keisha breathless. Fonnie grinned at her when Keisha tossed the blue fringed shawl from around her shoulders and gyrated her hips.

On the other hand Brian and Melanie seemed to prefer the slower steps. In fact, at one point, Fonnie feared they'd forgotten they were in full view on the dance floor. The only things that seemed to be moving were the charms on Melanie's bracelet as she walked her fingers across Brian's shoulder. Fonnie breathed a sigh of relief when they started moving their feet again.

Jeremiah whisked her around the room a few times,

but Fonnie was soon out of breath and decided to sit out the rest of the evening.

On the far side of the room, Edgar appeared to be having a deep conversation with Tony while Clara dragged Hank Peacock to his feet to dance. Doris kept time with her right foot and Lula kept busy refilling her glass.

As the band changed from one tempo to another, Edgar glanced over to the dance floor, and apparently remembering his duties as host, he rose, went over and pulled Midge to her feet. The two of them glided by Fonnie like dancers in an old musical.

"For a big man," Fonnie remarked to Jeremiah, "Edgar is certainly light on his feet."

"That he is. Comes from playing tennis." Jeremiah got up. "If you'll excuse me for a little while, I think I'll ask Lula to dance while she can still stand up. She's a nice gal, but I do wish she'd practice some moderation."

Fonnie motioned him away. "I'm fine. I enjoy looking at all the others." She watched as Edgar took Midge back to her seat and then stole Melanie away from Brian. Brian looked dejected for a moment, but soon recovered and asked Doris to dance. Edgar swung Melanie around as if she were a rag doll, and Melanie gave him a huge smile as she got into the rhythm.

Fonnie remembered fondly the days when she was young and willowy and could dance the night away. Now she was content to sit and watch. A phrase of Solomon's scooted through her brain, "To every thing there is a season." She accepted that and was thankful for her memories.

She continued to watch as partners were changed and the band played on. Buzz claimed Melanie, Brian pulled Midge to her feet, and Tony collected Keisha.

Edgar joined his wife at the bar, but didn't ask her to dance. Lula raised her glass in his direction, but Fonnie couldn't help but notice how sad she looked. Fonnie surmised that Lula would be glad when all the wedding guests were gone and she and Edgar would be alone to enjoy their beach home. Maybe then he would pay more attention to her.

When the music stopped again, Edgar made his way across the room and asked Keisha to dance. She'd been enjoying herself, but she was glad when the band started up on a slower beat. Edgar enfolded her in his strong arms, and he glided her effortlessly around the floor. Her long thin fingers rested against his short beefy ones. She was surprised when she felt calluses on the palm of his hand. It reminded her of her brother's hands. Tyrone earned extra money by doing yard work and it showed on his hands. She guessed Edgar had the hands of a sailor. She'd heard how much he loved his boats. In contrast, Stephon's and Tony's hands were both as smooth as polished wood.

He bent his head to speak to her. "I understand you and Fonnie are staying a few days."

"Yes. She wants to stay and enjoy the beach. This is the first chance she's had to travel in a couple of years."

"Good. Maybe you'll let me take you out on my boat."

Keisah nodded her head. "That'll be fun." She wasn't sure he meant the "you" as singular or plural, but that part could be straightened out later on. "What kind of boat do you have?"

"A small cabin cruiser. She's not fancy, but she's fast."

The music stopped and Stephon hurried to her side. Edgar thanked Keisha for the dance and turned around as Buzz clapped for attention.

Buzz had been going strong all evening: drinking, dancing, talking, and drinking some more. Now he stood up and raised his glass. "To all of us," he shouted. "May we all be lucky in life and lucky in love!"

Stephon gave Keisha a quick squeeze, and she smiled in return. Brian made his way over to Melanie as everyone started clapping.

Buzz brought his glass down and took another sip. As he did, the glass slid out of his hand and crashed to the floor. He leaned his head forward and stared at the splinters.

He let out a long groan. Then his body crumpled, and he fell, face down to the floor.

# SIX

MELANIE REACHED the collapsed man first. Fonnie watched as expert fingers searched for a carotid pulse, saw her nod as she found one. Brian was right behind her punching 911 on his cell phone. Fonnie hurried forward with the intention of playing nurse to the fallen man. She changed her mind when she saw how well Melanie and Brian were handling the situation.

Together they turned Buzz over onto his back. He was breathing, although his breaths were shallow. His eyes were closed, his face ashen. Melanie signaled Brian to grab a cushion from a nearby couch and they slid it under Buzz's head. Brian loosened Buzz's tie and unbuttoned the top of his shirt. Melanie made a finger-sweep of the victim's mouth to be sure nothing was obstructing his airway. Fonnie stood back and gazed in admiration at the young nurse and the young cop.

The other guests and waiters thronged around, hands over their mouths in concern or shaking their heads in bewilderment.

"I'm so glad Amy and Paul left earlier," Fonnie muttered to herself. "What a terrible way for a wedding reception to end."

Edgar ran over to his partner and dropped down beside him. "Buzz, can you hear me?"

Melanie gently shoved Edgar aside. "Just let me handle it. An ambulance is on the way."

"Thank God, you're here," Edgar said. He moved away to give her room.

Midge started elbowing through the crowd. "What the hell happened?" She made her way next to her husband's fallen body, peered over Melanie's shoulder and shouted, "Buzz, get your butt up off the floor. We're going to our room."

Melanie turned and spoke softly but firmly to Midge. "Mrs. Garrison, your husband isn't going anywhere—except to the hospital. I think he's had a heart attack. Now if you and everyone else will get out of the way, we'll try to keep him alive until the ambulance gets here."

"You can't talk to me like that. I've never liked you and I don't like you now. You think you know everything. It's ridiculous to say Buzz had a heart attack. His heart is as strong as a horse." Midge shoved the young nurse out of the way, slipped down to her knees, bent over her husband, and slapped him gently on his face. "Come on, Buzz Honey. Open those pretty brown eyes." Her voice caught and she wiped a tear from her cheek. "Please wake up. You're scaring the shit out of me."

Brian knelt down by the distraught woman and put his arm around her shoulders. "I know you're upset, Mrs. Garrison, but Melanie knows what she's doing." He glanced back at Fonnie and motioned her forward. "Why don't you sit down with Gram? We'll take good care of Buzz until the medics arrive."

Melanie reached across Midge and again took Buzz's pulse. "It's weaker and his breathing is slower. We might have to do CPR."

Fonnie stepped over to Midge's side and took her by the arm. "You'll be more help to Buzz if you join me in a prayer. Come on. The ambulance will be here soon."

Midge looked at Fonnie blankly, but nodded slowly and rose to her feet.

Fonnie led her to a corner sofa and Keisha brought her a glass of water. "Anything I can do?" Keisha asked. Fonnie shook her head Midge rubbed her hands together. Her pudgy fingers paused over the diamonds on her left hand. "It's impossible. There's nothing wrong with Buzz's heart. I don't understand how this could happen."

"Maybe his flu, or whatever he had, along with a little too much to drink precipitated an attack." Fonnie said. "But he's strong. He'll pull out of it."

Midge gave her a brave smile. "Sure. My Buzz is too stubborn to die."

EDGAR LED THE EMTs over to their patient. "For God's sake, hurry up. The man's dying."

Melanie rose and gave way to the two men with the stretcher and their medical bag. She patted Edgar on the arm. "It's all right. They need to get an IV started and give him oxygen. Then they can move him."

Fonnie reassured Midge. "They're doing exactly what has to be done."

"I want to ride in the ambulance with him." Midge choked back tears, grabbed a napkin from a nearby table, and blew her nose. "I want to be near him."

"Of course you do, but it'll be better if you ride to the hospital with Brian and me. You don't want to get in their way."

Fonnie studied the two young men as they calmly, competently went about their work. Everyone seems so young these days, she thought. Those boys hardly looked old enough to drive and here they were saving lives.

Edgar, Melanie, and Brian accompanied them as they headed out the door. Fonnie heard Edgar speak to the EMTs as they filed past. "Melanie's an RN. Works CCU. I want her to ride in the back with Buzz."

The one who looked the older of the two shrugged. "I don't know about that, sir. Is she family?"

"She's a close friend and your patient is my law partner. I want her with him. Understand?"

Melanie flashed a smile at the young men. "I promise I won't get in the way. I'll just scrunch up in back. You won't even know I'm there."

The youngest of the medics smiled back. "Sure. No problem. Let's go." As the gurney rolled toward the front door, he turned back and stared at Melanie in her skin-tight blue sheath and added, "But, I'll know you're there."

Brian hustled Midge and Fonnie out to his car. Keisha ran up as they were helping Midge into the back seat. "Want me to come along?"

Fonnie shook her head. "No need. I'll call when we find out something. Got your cell phone with you?"

"I'll get it and if you need me, be sure to call." Keisha reached in and pressed Midge's hand. "I'm praying for him. My pop's a preacher and he says prayer is powerful."

Midge sniffed and squeezed her hand. "Thank you."

Brian had the car in reverse when Jeremiah came running up. He tapped on the driver's window and Brian rolled it down. "Got room for me?" Jeremiah asked.

"Sure. Jump in."

Jeremiah raced around to the passenger side and scooted in. "I'm still the best man," he said, "and I have to know what's going on so I can report to Paul."

Fonnie poked him in the shoulder. "You're not going to report anything to Paul until the honeymooners are back home. There's no need to upset them when there's nothing they can do."

"That's right," Midge said. "And by the time they get home, Buzz will be all right."

Keisha watched as Brian drove off followed closely by Edgar and Hank and their wives. Stephon came up and put his arm around her shoulders. "You're shivering. Let's go inside."

"It *is* getting chilly. Or maybe it's just the thought of the closeness of death. I really don't think Buzz is going to make it. He looked terrible."

"Yeah." He gave her a hug. "Let's find some hot coffee."

They paused at the reception room entry. Band members were putting away their instruments, waiters were clearing tables, the janitor was sweeping up the broken glass. "I guess the coffee's gone," Stephon said. He shook his head, "I'm glad the newlyweds weren't here to see how their party ended."

"I know. What a shame." They were well past the door when Keisha suddenly stopped and turned back. "My shawl. I left it somewhere in there. I better find it."

"Go ahead. It looks like the coffee shop is about to close. I'll grab us a couple of cups to go."

Keisha made her way across the now empty dance floor, looked on chairs and under tables for her discarded shawl, and finally spied something blue on the floor by the bandstand. She picked it up, wrapped it tightly around her arms. It's warmth felt good and brought her a measure of comfort. On her way out she nearly stepped on a large piece of glass the janitor must have missed. She picked it up and looked for a trash can to put it in. Not finding one, she snatched a napkin from a table and wrapped the jagged piece of glass. She slid it into her pocket, intending to dispose of it as soon as possible.

Stephon sat on a couch in the lobby holding two foam cups. "Get it while it's hot. There's no more where this came from."

"Thanks. But do you mind if I run to my room first? I promised Fonnie I'd carry my cell phone in case she calls. I better go get it."

"I could go with you. We could enjoy our coffee in the privacy of your room."

Keisha hesitated then gave him a wide smile. "I think not. You stay here and enjoy warm thoughts. I'm going to change into jeans and sweat shirt and will be right back."

Stephon shrugged. "Whatever."

As she slipped off her dress, Keisha remembered the fragment of Buzz's glass she'd picked up. She looked for her waste basket, but not seeing it immediately, she slid the piece of glass into the drawer of the bedside stand. Her thoughts stayed on Stephon as she freshened her lipstick and ran a comb through her hair.

When she returned to the lobby, Keisha noticed Stephon had also changed into jeans. He was talking to a couple who were checking out. They were friends of Amy's that Keisha had met the day before although she couldn't recall their names. The woman was pacing impatiently as her husband signed the credit card receipt. "I'm so upset," she said to Stephon. "I told Tom I couldn't stand to spend another night here. I don't think that man had a heart attack. He's been sick ever since we arrived. He may be dying from some horrible disease, and the sooner we get out the better. It's just not safe around here."

The man turned from the desk and rolled his eyes at Stephon. "She's got quite an imagination, but there's no use arguing with her."

Stephon nodded, reached out and shook his hand. "Have a good trip back."

Keisha smiled as Stephon joined her in front of the gas logs burning brightly in the fireplace. She sipped her coffee and wiggled her sneakered feet at the flames. "Almost cozy."

"Almost," Stephon said. "If you can forget we're in a public lobby with the night clerk keeping a close eye on us. And worse yet, she reminds me of my grandmother."

"Better your grandmother than mine." Keisha slid closer and slipped her hand into his. "Thanks for being here. You're good company. But I really think I should go to the hospital. Fonnie may need me."

"Why? She has Brian—and Melanie."

Keisha's smile turned upside down. "I know."

"What's wrong?"

"There's something about Melanie that rubs me the wrong way."

Stephon's eyebrows shot up. "What? She's beautiful, competent, sweet. Fonnie and Brian both like her. You're not jealous, are you?"

"Don't be ridiculous." Keisha took another sip of coffee. "But just the same, I'll feel better if I go to the hospital."

"Fine. I'll drive you."

"That's not necessary. I can go by myself."

"Sure you can, but I'd like to go with you. You're beautiful and sweet too—and I like being with you."

Keisha leaned over and kissed him on the cheek. "You're the sweet one."

Stephon gave her a quick hug. "We'd better be careful. That grandma at the desk is eyeing us."

# SEVEN

A WOMAN WAS STANDING outside the ER door. Her head rested against the "No Smoking" sign, and a cigarette dangled from her fingers. She lifted her head up to greet Keisha and Stephon. "Two more to stand vigil over the sick."

"Hello, Lula," Keisha said. "Have you heard any news yet?"

"Nary a word. The patient had already been whisked away to the inner sanctum when we got here and nobody's come out since."

"How is Midge doing?"

"Not good. Buzz and Midge fussed a lot, but she really loves him. This is hard on her."

"I'm sure it is," Keisha said.

"And Edgar's going out of his mind," Lula added. "You'd think Buzz was his brother instead of just a partner."

"I can understand that," Stephon said. "The people you work with can become closer than your own family."

Lula laughed. "I wouldn't know about that. Edgar loves to remind me that I've never really worked a day in my life. As if trying to keep him happy isn't a full time job." She took a deep drag of her cigarette. "God, I wish I had a drink. I should have snatched a bottle and brought it with me." She ran her fingers up Stephon's arm. "Think you could find me a little something?"

Stephon shook his head. "Sorry. Small towns like this close the bars just before they roll up the sidewalks."

Keisha took him by the hand. "Come on. We'd better go in."

Lula waved her right index finger at them. "That's right, Honey, keep a close eye on your man. If, by any chance, Edgar is looking for me, tell him I'll be in shortly." She brought the cigarette to her lips, then called after them. "Oh, by the way, I've convinced Edgar to apply for a liquor license for the motel. Won't that be great?"

"Sure," Stephon answered. "At least, it'll be convenient."

Keisha jerked on his hand as the automatic door opened. "Poor Edgar," she said.

"Poor Edgar, is right. She'll drink up all his profits before he knows what's happening."

THE WAITING ROOM was packed. Keisha glanced around for Fonnie. She was sitting in a chair closest to the double doors labeled "Staff Only." Midge and Doris sat next to her. Brian and Melanie stood in a far corner, apparently oblivious to everyone else. Edgar paced, Hank had slid down in a chair and seemed to be dozing. Jeremiah sat by himself, looking lonely and dejected.

In another corner, a Latino couple clung to each other, and an older man sobbed against a young woman's shoulder. Keisha's heart went out to everyone in the room. It was a side of herself she tried hard to hide from others. She'd figured out long ago that she and Fonnie had this in common—a tender heart paired with a tough facade.

She glanced over to where Fonnie and Midge sat. Fonnie caught her eye and beckoned her over. Keisha dropped Stephon's hand. "I'm going to check on Fonnie."

Stephon nodded, smiled over at the women. "I'll wait here for you."

Keisha bent down and touched Midge's hand. Fonnie didn't give her a chance to say anything. "See that pink-lady over there?" Fonnie motioned somewhere down an adjoining hall.

Keisha looked in that direction and noted the volunteer in a pink pinafore. "Yes. What about her?"

"See if she can get you a box of tissues. Midge has gone through all of mine and is now working on a wad of toilet paper I grabbed from the bathroom. I don't know which is running worse—her eyes or her nose."

Midge lifted blood-shot eyes, gave Keisha a wan smile, and sniffed. "I'm sorry. Fonnie's doing her best to cheer me up, but I just can't help myself. It's my fault. I should have made him see a doctor when he first got sick."

"Nonsense," Fonnie said. "It's not your fault." She dropped a clump of matted material in a nearby trash can.

"I'll get some tissues." Keisha walked over to the pink lady. On her way, she passed Brian and Melanie and couldn't help overhearing some of their conversation.

"Are you sure you have to leave in the morning?" Melanie asked in a deep whisper reminiscent of an old Lauren Bacall movie.

"Yes," Brian whispered back, "I have to leave in the morning. Duty calls."

"But you'll call me?"

"You know I will. Often."

Keisha slowed her steps and brushed some imaginary dirt off her sweatshirt sleeve. But the whispers became softer and she couldn't hear anything else. She glanced up, saw Fonnie glaring at her, and hurried to get the box of tissues.

Fonnie snatched the box and motioned over to Jeremiah. "Why don't you and Stephon sit by Jeremiah? I hate to see him all alone like that, but I think I need to stay with Midge."

Keisha nodded her agreement.

Fonnie reached across Midge and tapped Doris on the arm. "I wonder why Clara and Tony didn't come." As Paul's daughter, Fonnie thought the girl should be concerned about her father's partner. "Did you see them when you left the motel?"

"They were in the lobby when we left," Doris said. "I heard Clara tell him that it was a shame that her dad's wedding day had to end in a disaster. Then Tony said something about most weddings ending in disaster."

"What an odd remark," Fonnie said.

Doris went on. "He laughed like he was making a joke, but Clara didn't seem to think it was funny. She said they ought to go to the hospital, but he said he was going up to bed. Then he hurried toward for the elevator. When we went out the door, she was rushing down the hall after him."

"Nothing they could do here anyway, but still...."

Fonnie's voice trailed off as she stood up to stretch.

She wasn't accustomed to sitting in a straight-back chair. Her back ached, her legs were cramping, her body longed for bed. She'd made a remarkable recovery from her stroke, but she still fatigued easily. As much as she bragged about being "as good as new," it wasn't completely true. Whenever she became overly tired, she could feel the weakness returning to her left side. But she couldn't think of herself now. She sat back down and took Midge's hand again.

At that moment, one side of the double doors opened. A white coat appeared. Fonnie raised her head and saw the troubled eyes behind the wire-rimmed glasses. The doctor walked over to them. His eyes paused on the woman clutching a handful of damp tissues. "Mrs. Garrison?"

Midge bobbed her head a quarter of an inch to acknowledge her identity and tightened her grip on Fonnie's hand.

Fonnie knew what the doctor's next words would be.

"I'm sorry. We did all we could."

Midge closed her eyes, started rocking back and forth on the metal chair. Doris slipped her arm around her and hugged her close.

Melanie and Edgar both seemed to notice the doctor at the same time. Edgar stopped his pacing in mid-stride and dashed across the room. Melanie strode over quickly.

"What is it?" Edgar demanded.

"We did all we could, sir, but Mr. Garrison didn't make it."

Edgar swerved around, screwed up his face in a picture of despair. He pounded his fist against the back of a chair. "Damn! Damn it all!"

The doctor turned back to Midge, but Melanie leaned forward. “Then it *was* a heart attack?”

“It appears it was a coronary event.”

Brian came up behind Melanie. She pivoted around, gave him a sad smile. “Poor Buzz. In the prime of his life. One never knows.”

The doctor turned back to Midge. She stared up at him. “It’s hard to believe. And I thought he just had the flu.”

“As I said, it appears to have been a coronary event, but the origin of it isn’t clear. He’d been sick?”

“Well, yes. That is, he kept complaining of nausea and stomach cramps and some dizziness. But today he was feeling better.”

Fonnie released Midge’s hand, stood up, and motioned for the doctor to take her seat.

He sat down, touched Midge’s arm. “Mrs. Garrison, as with any unexpected death when the diagnosis is in question, an autopsy is indicated.”

Midge’s eyes welled up again and Fonnie shoved some more tissues at her. “Autopsy?”

“Yes. It’s important we discover the exact cause of death.”

Midge shook her head. “Why? It won’t bring him back.”

“It’s important for our medical knowledge—and for your peace of mind.”

“Now just a minute.” Edgar motioned Doris out of her chair next to Midge and plopped down in it himself. “Buzz Garrison was my law partner and my best friend. I’m not going to let you cut on him just to satisfy your curiosity.”

Fonnie noticed the withering look the doctor gave Edgar. She tried to maneuver closer to Midge to give her emotional support and back up the need for an autopsy. She didn't get the chance.

"Edgar is right," Midge said. "What difference does it make if it was a blocked artery or a blood clot or whatever? My Buzz is dead. All I want now is to take him home."

The doctor stood up, brushed back his hair. Fonnie could tell he was trying to control his temper. When he spoke, his voice was low but determined. "I'm afraid it's not that simple, Mrs. Garrison. The hospital has certain guidelines for situations like this. I can't sign the death certificate without a definite diagnosis." He paused. "I'm sure you understand."

Midge shook her head. "No, I don't understand." She paused. "But I guess there's nothing I can do about it."

"I'll have someone bring out the papers for you to sign." The doctor disappeared behind the double doors.

"Blasted bureaucracy," Edgar said. "Give me ten minutes and I can put a stop to this nonsense. Hospital guidelines, my foot. He can't force you to sign those papers."

"Thank you, dear Edgar. But there's no need to raise such a fuss. Let them do their thing if they have to. Then we'll take Buzz home and give him the memorial service he deserves."

"Are you sure you're all right with the autopsy?"

"Yes. It's okay."

"Then as soon as you sign the damn permit, Lula and I are taking you back to the motel. You'll stay in our suite tonight. We have an extra bedroom."

Fonnie tried to regain her chair next to Midge, but this time Melanie scooted into it. "Don't worry. They just have to do the autopsy to satisfy the hospital review committee. It won't take long and by tomorrow you'll be free to take your husband home for burial."

Midge gave Melanie a questioning stare. "You mean they won't check everything?"

"This is just a small hospital. They'll only do what they have to."

Midge sat up straighter and smiled at Melanie. "I'm sorry I snapped at you earlier. I was just upset. Thank you for trying to help Buzz."

A secretary came up and asked Midge to step behind the counter. Fonnie watched as a nurse apparently explained the autopsy permit and Midge signed it. The two witnesses then also signed. When Midge came out, Edgar took her elbow and propelled her out of the waiting room.

Brian came up to Fonnie. "Do you mind if you and Jeremiah ride back with Keisha and Stephon. I'm going to take Melanie. She's pretty wrung out. We may drive up the coast a ways."

"That'll be fine. She's had a rough night. A relaxing ride would do her good."

The waiting room started to empty out. Keisha came up to Fonnie. "Ready to go?"

They went out the door at the same time as Hank and Doris. "What a night," Hank said. "Wish I could turn back time. Last week Buzz and I were enjoying Florida sunshine, playing golf, sipping drinks, not a care in the world."

Doris pursed up her lips. "I don't know about that," she said.

Fonnie looked surprised. “What do you mean?”

“I mean Buzz didn’t strike me as being all that carefree. I remember mentioning to Midge that he seemed worried about something.”

“And what did Midge say about that?” Fonnie asked.

“She said I was imagining it.”

# EIGHT

FONNIE SPENT a fitful night. Bits of scenes and conversations from the evening before played hide-and-seek in her head. It wasn't just because a man had died unexpectedly. Fonnie was no stranger to death. She knew sudden death happened—to the young, the old, the strong, the vigorous, as well as to the sickly. However, she couldn't help but wonder if Buzz's earlier illness had anything to do with his death, and why Midge initially opposed the autopsy.

She threw off the covers, slid into her slippers, and padded over to the window. She pulled back the drapes and gazed at the calm, glistening water. The morning beach beckoned her. Well, she had come here to walk the sands. She might as well get started. Maybe a good stroll was what she needed to still the nagging voice in her head—a voice trying to tell her something wasn't quite right.

As Fonnie started to turn around, a flash of pink appeared in her peripheral vision. She studied the slight figure as it jogged closer across the sand. It was Melanie in a pink sweat suit. Her blonde hair, tied back in a pony tail, swished back and forth like a real pony's tail swatting flies. Fonnie sighed. Oh, for the energy to be able to run again.

She made a quick trip to the bathroom, pulled on a pair of slacks, a heavy sweater, and her walking shoes. Maybe she could catch Melanie when the girl finished her run and discuss some things with her. Fonnie felt it would ease her mind to talk to someone. She knew Brian had left for home early that morning and Keisha was probably sleeping in. Fonnie had heard her come in late last night. She assumed Keisha and Stephon had either gone for a drive or had a late night chat.

Fonnie took a short walk on the beach then waited on the verandah until she sighted Melanie heading back toward the motel. She waved as Melanie sprinted up the steps. The young girl wiggled her pony tail and smiled. "Nothing like a brisk run to work up an appetite," Fonnie said. "How about joining me for breakfast?"

"I'd love to."

A short while later Fonnie was comparing her scrambled eggs, sausage patty, and two buttered biscuits with Melanie's grapefruit juice and one piece of dry toast. "You call that breakfast? My parakeet used to eat more than that." Fonnie bit into a biscuit, swiped some butter off her lips. "Come to think of it, the vet said he died from starvation."

Melanie gave the obligatory laugh. "You have such a sense of humor."

"It's just a front. I'm really a miserable old witch who didn't get much sleep last night."

Melanie instantly looked concerned. "And why couldn't you sleep?"

That was the opening Fonnie was hoping for and she took advantage of it. "I'm worried about what the coroner might find on Buzz's autopsy."

Melanie nibbled at her toast and took a drink of juice before responding. "Whatever do you mean?"

"I don't know. It's just that at first Midge was against having an autopsy done. I thought that strange. If it had been my husband, I would've insisted on a post-mortem—would want to find out exactly what killed him. But she didn't seem to want to know." Fonnie sipped her coffee. "Then there was Doris's remark."

Melanie took another bite of toast. "And what did Doris say?"

"That Buzz had seemed upset when they were in Florida, but Midge denied it."

"Oh. Is that all? Aunt Doris has always been a worrywart. She makes a habit of seeing evil omens and of prophesying bad luck. She's never happier than when she can alarm someone."

Melanie toyed with her toast, breaking it into tiny pieces. "And that business about Midge not wanting an autopsy. That's only natural. A lot of people hate to think of their loved ones being cut up. They seem to think it violates the body. Of course, you and I know it's purely a medical procedure. Midge will be all right. She isn't one to sit around and mope."

"Then you know her well?" Fonnie asked.

"Sure. She and Buzz vacationed every year with Uncle Hank and Aunt Doris in Miami. I visited them often. When Stephon was there last week, the six of us went night clubbing together."

Fonnie's fork stopped midway to her mouth and she let it fall back on her plate. "Stephon was in Miami?"

Melanie nodded as she downed the rest of her grapefruit juice.

"That's why I came up here. Stephon asked me to. He was afraid it was going to be boring for him and he wanted someone his own age around. So I thought, why not? He's a really nice guy, but when I met your grandson, I forgot all about Stephon." Melanie giggled like a school girl. "I guess it's just as well, the way Stephon's been making time with Keisha."

Fonnie shook her head in dismay. "Making time?"

"You know what I mean. I thought at first he just took up with her because I went for Brian, but I think he's got it bad. I guess your generation would say that Stephon is smitten with Keisha."

Fonnie glanced up and was so very glad to see someone from her generation. Jeremiah was heading toward their table. Thank goodness. She didn't think she could take much more of this conversation. Her thoughts were more confusing now than they had been during the night. Did Brian know Melanie had dated Stephon? Did Keisha know? Did it matter? Was it even considered a date, if the two of them had just gone night clubbing with a group?

Melanie jumped up as Jeremiah joined them. "Got to get changed," she said. "Edgar's taking me out on his boat this morning. Lula hates boats. I can't imagine why she agreed to live at the beach."

Jeremiah pulled up an empty chair. His face was serious. "I know what you said last night, but I really do have to call Paul and tell him about Buzz."

"Yes, of course. He must be told about the death of one of his partners. But why don't you wait until after the autopsy report when the funeral arrangements are announced? I know they'll want to fly back for the service."

Jeremiah signaled a waiter and asked for coffee and a bagel.

"Is that all you're having?" Fonnie asked.

A smile lit up Jeremiah's face. "Are you kidding? I've been up for hours. Took an early morning swim and ate a breakfast big enough for loggers. This is my mid-morning snack. I looked for you earlier. Glad you finally decided to crawl out of bed."

"I'll have you know I've been up quite a while and even walked a little on the beach."

"Nothing like brisk sea air to clear the mind and soothe the spirit."

"I don't know about that. My mind is a jumbled mess and my spirit isn't much better. I was worried about Midge when I woke up, and now I'm concerned about Brian and about Keisha."

"Tell me all about it. I'm a good listener."

Fonnie did her best to explain why Melanie's remarks about Stephon upset her. "I'm sure she didn't tell Brian she came up here to be with Stephon, and I'm positive Keisha is in the dark about any relationship between him and Melanie."

Jeremiah finished his coffee, pushed back from the table, smiled at Fonnie. "Before we get any further into this soap opera, let's step outside. The swing in the gazebo seems to be beckoning us."

"Sounds good to me," Fonnie said.

The swing faced the ocean, and Fonnie had to shade her eyes from the sun as it rose higher in the sky. The temperature was in the fifties with a slight breeze. The gulls kept up a lively chatter with each other as they swooped and dipped for their breakfast while the gentle rhythm of the surf played in the background. Fonnie pulled her sweater closer and turned her face from the sun to Jeremiah. "A little chilly, but beautiful for this time of year. Too bad I can't just relax and enjoy it."

"You worry too much. The young people will be fine. If there are problems, they'll work on them. If they can't work them out, they'll bounce back and go on with their lives. Kids today are tough and resilient."

"You think?"

"I know. Take my grand-niece, Clara. She's in a troubled marriage. I was concerned about her and we talked. Know what she told me?"

"Now that's a rhetorical question if ever I heard one."

Jeremiah grinned and smoothed back his hair that was playing tag with the wind. "She said she was going to work on it, give him a chance to straighten up and fly right, and if he didn't, she'd move on."

"Brave talk, but I doubt it's that easy."

"I know it's not, especially since she's expecting."

"Clara's pregnant? I didn't know that. Do Amy and Paul know they're going to be grandparents?"

"She told the family a few days ago. She's only a couple of months along." Jeremiah pushed the swing back and forth a few times before going on. "She's determined to have the baby with or without Tony. Whatever happens, she'll be all right. As I said, young people are tough and resilient. Keisha will be fine, and so will Brian. You have to let them find their own way."

"You're right. And I think I need to get better acquainted with Clara. She sounds like she's got a real head on her shoulders. What does she do? I don't recall Paul saying."

"She's a librarian—a genuine bibliophile."

"A woman after my own heart. And Tony?"

"The only thing he reads is the financial page. He's an investment broker. Paul thinks he's pretty smart. He handles investments for all the partners."

"Well, as the old saying goes—opposites attract. I wish them my best." The wind picked up a little and Fonnie shivered. "But it's harder to be resilient when we get older. I wonder how Midge will do."

"A good looking, financially-secure widow in her fifties? Give her a few months and she'll be riding high."

"Providing there's no surprise on the autopsy."

Jeremiah braked the swing to an abrupt halt. "Why do you say that?"

"I don't know. Just a gut feeling. I can't put my finger on it. It's the same kind of feeling I had when my roommate at the nursing home died. The doctor there said it was a heart attack."

"And it wasn't?"

Fonnie shook her head. "It was murder."

"Wow!"

"Yeah, wow. But in this case, I hope I'm wrong."

"The autopsy was scheduled for this morning. Surely they'll let Midge know something by this afternoon."

"But how will I know? I'm not family or even a close friend."

"Edgar will insist on finding out since he's head of the firm, and Edgar will have to tell me so I can keep Paul informed. Then I'll tell you. Okay?"

"That'll work."

# NINE

KEISHA STRETCHED, grinned, rolled over and hugged her pillow. Snatches of a song she'd heard recently on TV jiggled in her head. It was from an old musical whose title she couldn't recall but she sang some of the words softly. "It's a grand night for singing. The stars are bright above. La la la. And I think I am falling in love." She threw the pillow on the floor, dashed to the window, and sang to the gentle waves. "Falling, falling in love."

She ran over to the dresser and peered into the mirror. "Yes, Keisha Riggs. I think you're in love." She snatched up her shawl from a chair and twirled around the room.

She took her time getting dressed, added a little mascara to her already thick lashes, put on her brightest lipstick. She was ready to greet this beautiful day.

Stephon was waiting for her in the lobby with a smile as big as New York. "I called my office. They can do without me until after the weekend. And since Monday is Presidents' Day, it'll be a long weekend." He reached over and grasped her hand. "What do you think about that?"

Keisha curled her fingers around his. "I think it was very considerate of George and Abe to have February birthdays. I always did like those guys."

"I just saw Fonnie with Jeremiah in the gazebo.

Maybe he'll keep her busy so we can spend some time alone. How about a leisurely stroll down the beach?"

"Fine, but maybe I'd better go back to my room and get a jacket. I see some dark clouds coming in."

A LIGHT RAIN drove Fonnie and Jeremiah out of the gazebo back to the motel. Jeremiah suggested they take a drive up the coast. "No use moping around waiting for the autopsy report. We can take a leisurely ride, stop somewhere for lunch, then meander back."

"Sounds good. Let me go to my room and freshen up and see what Keisha has in mind."

She spied Keisha by the elevator and called out for her to wait. Keisha grinned as Fonnie hurried to get in the door. "My daddy once told me never to run after an elevator or a man," Keisha said. "There would always be another one coming along."

"Wise words. I hope you heed them. But I was hurrying so I could talk to you."

"Talk away."

"Jeremiah and I are going for a ride. Want to come along?"

"Thanks, but no thanks. Stephon and I decided to walk the beach, but if it starts raining, we may watch a movie in his room."

Fonnie nearly bit her tongue to avoid giving the young girl some grandmotherly advice. Instead she said, "That's nice. It'll give you a chance to get better acquainted. You probably have questions about his background."

The elevator door opened and Keisha followed Fonnie down the hall. Keisha unlocked her door, paused, motioned Fonnie in. "I know all I need to know about Stephon, but you apparently have some questions. So come in and ask away. If I know the answer, I'll tell you and if not, I'll find out."

"It's really none of my business but...."

"That's right. But you're nosy."

Fonnie flounced into the room and dropped into the easy chair. "I like to know about people. That's all."

"Okay. Here's a brief bio. Stephon is one of seven children. His siblings are scattered throughout the South. His parents live in Wheeling. He graduated from UVA. He likes his work. He admires Amy. And he intends to make it big in real estate. Anything else you want to know?"

"Does he travel much in his real estate ventures?"

Keisha gave Fonnie a puzzled look. "Just around the Richmond area I guess. He's only licensed in Virginia."

So, Fonnie thought, what was he doing in Florida last week? And had he mentioned it to Keisha? If so, she gave no indication of it. "Well," Fonnie said. "It's nice he can get some vacation time. I remember when Amy started in the business, she seldom was able to take time off. But I guess things change."

"I don't know about that. He's planning on staying here through President's Day. Then he has to get back to the office." Keisha put on some fresh lipstick and a smile. "Now I'm sure Jeremiah is waiting for you and I know Stephon is waiting for me. Want to meet up for dinner about six?"

Fonnie nodded as she headed for her own room.

WHEN JEREMIAH and Fonnie returned from their ride, she retreated to her room for a nap and Jeremiah went in search of Edgar to find out if he had any news of the autopsy report. They planned to meet back in the dining room.

Fonnie went down early. She wanted to be sure to be there when Jeremiah brought the news. The room was filling up with guests arriving for the three-day weekend. Brian had told her February was not a good beach month, but there seemed to be a lot of people who didn't agree with him. Or maybe some folks figured any holiday was a good excuse to leave home.

She commandeered a table near the verandah where she could look out to the rolling surf. The rain had stopped and the fading daylight was glistening on the water. The beach is lovely, she thought, no matter what time of year it is.

She glanced up to see Clara entering the room alone. Fonnie waved, got Clara's attention and motioned her over. "You're alone?" Fonnie asked.

Clara gave a weak smile. "Looks like. Tony said he was going jogging an hour ago and hasn't gotten back. He probably got to talking with somebody. I've been busy packing. We plan on going home in the morning." She pulled out a chair. "May I join you?"

Fonnie nodded. "Please do. I'm expecting your uncle momentarily as well as Keisha and Stephon. When Tony comes, we can make room for him."

Clara sat down and clasped her hands in front of her. "I'm glad Jeremiah's made a friend here. You two make a nice couple."

"I enjoy his company," Fonnie said. "He's certainly not boring." She paused, reached over and grasped Clara's hands. "And he told me your good news. Since

I'm your father's mother-in-law, will the baby make me an official great-grandmother?"

"Absolutely. That is, if that's the way you want it."

"Of course, that's the way I want it. Everybody is going to be thrilled with that baby."

Clara bent her head and said softly. "I hope you're right."

Before Fonnie could answer, she saw Keisha, Stephon, and Jeremiah coming toward the table. The two young people were smiling at each other as if they were sharing a delicious secret. Jeremiah looked worried.

The three of them greeted Clara. "Where's Tony?" Stephon asked as he pulled out Keisha's chair and then seated himself.

Clara shrugged. "I suspect he'll be along shortly."

Fonnie immediately turned her attention to Jeremiah. She didn't even wait for him to get seated before she asked, "Any news?"

He dropped into his chair and took a deep breath. "Afraid so."

His brief answer got the attention of everyone at the table. Keisha and Stephon stopped looking at each other and stared at the older man. Clara clenched her fists tighter.

Fonnie barely gave him a nanosecond to continue before she demanded, "What?"

"Edgar, acting as attorney for the next of kin, got the autopsy report. It only said that further examination was warranted. Blood and tissue samples are being sent to Chapel Hill to the state chief medical examiner."

Keisha shook her head. "I don't understand. What does that mean? Why would they need further tests?"

"It means they still can't determine the cause of death," Fonnie said. "And the state medical examiner can do more elaborate testing than can be done on the local level."

Stephon started playing with his silverware, then looked up at Fonnie, and asked, "Testing for what?"

A waitress came up, and the conversation halted. She placed menus and water on the table, and assured them she'd be right back to take their order.

Jeremiah nodded at her. "No hurry."

Keisha repeated Stephon's question, "What are they testing for?"

Fonnie shrugged. "I suppose anything unusual, something in his blood or tissues that shouldn't be there."

"Anything suspicious," Jeremiah added.

Stephon took a long drink of water, sat the glass down slowly. "You mean like—poison."

Clara gave a short laugh. "Don't be ridiculous, Stephon. Why would anyone want to poison Buzz Garrison? Everybody liked him."

Stephon propped his chin on his hand and let out a low, "Hmmm. Maybe not everybody."

Keisha stared at him. "What are you talking about?"

"Maybe little Midge got tired of all his whining and decided to put him out of his misery."

"How can you say such a horrible thing? Midge is heartbroken over Buzz's death." Keisha turned to Fonnie. "You were there with her when the doctor came out. You saw how upset she was."

"Yes. It was a great shock to her." Fonnie took a sip of water. "She loved him. I could tell that."

"You wouldn't say that if you'd seen how they

bickered all the time," Stephon said. "Let me tell you they were not loveydovey."

"Oh? You spent a lot time with them?" If Stephon's visit in Miami was completely innocent, Fonnie thought, then now was his chance to mention it. He could tell them about nightclubbing with Buzz and Midge and Melanie. She waited. He didn't mention Florida at all.

"No. Not really. I had drinks with them a couple of times after I played golf with Buzz. But all that time she was bitching about one thing or the other. And Buzz wasn't shy about throwing it back at her."

Jeremiah nodded. "He's right. Paul invited me to a couple of parties that included his partners and their wives. Midge and Buzz were not poster children for a happy marriage. I guess they stayed together out of habit or convenience or stubbornness. Hard to tell."

Keisha threw up a hand like a cop stopping traffic. "Wait a minute. Aren't you two getting carried away? I admit I thought Midge was lacking in compassion about Buzz's illness, but when he died, I swear she was devastated."

"Let's forget about Midge for a minute," Fonnie said. "Jeremiah, was that all Edgar had to say about the autopsy?"

"Only that he was as mad as hell."

"Why would he be mad?" Clara asked.

"Edgar's a control freak. He likes to run things. He'd already scheduled the cremation and the memorial service. He told me that Midge asked him to take care of the details. She and Buzz had no children, and his only sister is in a nursing home. Edgar jumped on the assignment like he does most jobs. Now his plans are all screwed up and he's mad. Can't say that I blame him."

Clara frowned. "It seems to me that finding the truth should take precedence over a timetable. Did Edgar say when the final arrangements could go ahead?"

Jeremiah shook his head. "They told him that with the holiday weekend coming up, it might be next week before the body was released."

"Poor Midge," Keisha said. "The waiting will be hard on her."

Jeremiah picked up his menu as the waitress came toward them. "It's time to think about something more cheerful. I'm for whatever that delicious smell is coming from the kitchen."

Conversation stalled while their orders were being taken. Then Jeremiah started a discussion about the various lighthouses along the Carolina beaches. That was fine with Fonnie, and the others seemed glad to talk about something besides death and autopsies.

Clara kept up her end of the exchange, but Fonnie noticed she kept looking expectantly at the door. When the food arrived and Tony failed to appear, Clara ate quickly and then excused herself. "I'd better finish packing. Tony wants to leave early tomorrow." She smiled around the table. "It's been so nice meeting all of you."

Jeremiah stood up and gave her a hug. "I'll call you when I get back home. Maybe we can have lunch together."

"I'd like that."

Clara hadn't been gone long when Stephon pushed

back from the table. "Looks like the wind has died down some. Let's take that beach walk, Keisha, before it gets completely dark."

She slid her chair back. "Sure."

Jeremiah gave them a slight wave. "Maybe we could all get together later and play a little canasta."

Keisha hesitated. "Maybe. What do you think, Stephon?"

"I'm not much for cards. And I hear there's a club down the road with a pretty good band. We might give them a try." He looked over at Fonnie. "Want to shake a leg with us?"

"I'm afraid my legs wouldn't take your kind of music."

After the young people left, Jeremiah turned to Fonnie. "I really must call Paul tonight and fill him in."

"Yes, of course. But tell him they don't have to hurry back since the memorial service won't be until next week. And try not to worry him about—about the cause of death. We really don't know anything for sure."

"I'll be discreet. But just between you and me, what do you think?"

Fonnie turned her head and looked out the window at the lovely beach, the soft waves, the soaring gulls.

She leaned back in her chair, wiped her hand across her forehead. "I think Buzz was poisoned. And the murderer is here."

# TEN

FONNIE'S GAZE FOLLOWED Jeremiah as he left to call Paul and Amy. She hated that their honeymoon was going to be interrupted with the news of a death—an unexpected death—a suspicious death.

Her thoughts centered on the state medical examiner in Chapel Hill. What tests were being done? They had to be tests for a poisonous substance. Buzz hadn't been shot or beaten or smothered or drowned. Something had alerted the doctor or medical examiner here to the possibility of foul play. Fonnie wished she could have gotten closer to the victim last night. Maybe she would have noticed something. Skin discoloration, an odd odor, something. But if there had been anything suspicious, Melanie or Brian would have picked up on it.

Fonnie smiled as one of the people in her thoughts materialized in front of her face. "Melanie. I'm so glad you're here." She motioned for the younger woman to join her. "I was just going to have more coffee. Want some?"

Melanie sank into the chair opposite Fonnie, her hair windblown, her face sweaty, her eyes angry. "Might as well. Nothing else to do around this place except run and wait."

"You've been running again? There's such a thing as overdoing the exercise bit, you know."

"I know. But I'm so frustrated."

Fonnie assumed what she hoped was an innocent look and pretended not to know anything about the autopsy report. "Frustrated? About what?"

"You haven't heard? The two-bit, small-town medical examiner here can't make up his mind about Buzz's cause of death, so he's holding up the funeral in order to get a second opinion."

Melanie snapped her fingers at a passing waitress and ordered two coffees. "And make it fast. I'm tired of waiting around."

The waitress, chubby and fortyish, gave Fonnie the impression that she seldom did anything fast. She pushed back her glasses, took her time writing down the order, and asked, "Anything else."

Melanie shook her head and waved the waitress off. "And Brian was just as upset as I was when I told him about it."

"You talked to Brian?" Fonnie had thought about calling him but didn't know what time he'd get off duty tonight.

"Sure," Melanie said. Her eyes and face and voice all softened. "He called me on his way home. Said he missed—but then you're not interested in that. He agreed it was outrageous to waste the taxpayers' money doing useless autopsies."

That didn't sound like Brian, Fonnie thought. He was a cop. If there were the slightest doubt as to the cause of death, he'd want to learn the truth. Or was he so besotted by the beautiful Melanie, he'd agree to anything she said?

"But Melanie, you're so observant. Are you sure you didn't notice anything unusual about Buzz when he fell, or when he was in the ambulance?"

"Other than the fact that he was dying?"

"I mean anything that might indicate—poison?"

The waitress waddled up, set down two cups of coffee, emptied packets of cream and sweetener from her apron pocket, and slapped down the ticket. She gave Fonnie a bright smile. "Enjoy your coffee."

Melanie tore open two packs of artificial sweetener, dumped them into the hot brew and stirred it vigorously. Without looking up she echoed Fonnie's last word. "Poison?" She stirred some more and shook her head in rhythm with the spoon. "But that doesn't make sense. Why would she?" The young nurse caught her breath. "I mean, why would anybody do that?"

Fonnie noted the accusatory "she" Melanie had flung out, but decided not to comment on it. "That's what I was wondering. Who would want Buzz dead?" Fonnie lifted her cup, stared across the table. "In mysteries, now is when the detective asks, 'Who stood to gain by his death?'"

Melanie shrugged. "I suppose that would be Midge, if you're talking about life insurance. On the other hand, Paul might benefit a great deal from it."

"Paul?" Fonnie lowered her cup so quickly the coffee sloshed over the saucer and onto the table. She grabbed a napkin and swiped at the spill. "How on earth could it benefit Paul?"

"The law firm. It's Myers, Garrison, and Trent. Paul is the newest and youngest partner. It's no secret that Edgar Myers wants to retire early and become a beach bum. With Buzz Garrison out of the way, Paul Trent will be in the driver's seat. He'll be free to bring in some younger partners who can do all the work while he enjoys being top cat. How's that for a motive?"

"Insulting, appalling, and slanderous! How can you even think such a thing?"

"Whoa, Fonnie." Melanie put both hands in front of her face as if to ward off a blow. "I didn't say I thought that. I was just mentioning the possibility. Besides Paul had already left when Buzz collapsed." She took several sips of her coffee and then added, "But we both know some poisons are slow acting and that alcohol could disguise any bitter or odd taste."

Fonnie pushed back her chair. "I will not sit here and listen to disparaging remarks about my new son-in-law. Anybody could have slipped something into Buzz's drinks. Goodness knows he had enough of them."

"I know. And I'm sorry I upset you. I really wasn't serious about Paul. It's just that I hate for Midge to be the only valid suspect. If, of course, any poison is found. Personally, I still think the man died from a heart attack."

Fonnie felt a dark doubt creep into her mind along with the darkness that had fallen during their conversation. Only a few days ago when she had first met Stephon and then Melanie, she immediately liked both of them. Now she was having second thoughts. Wasn't anyone what they purported to be any more? She smiled at Melanie as she rose from the table. "I hope you're right. Then we can just go back to mourning the death of a fine man instead of looking for suspects in a murder case."

Even as she said the words, Fonnie knew there was little chance of that. She was convinced there had been, and probably still was, a murderer at the Beachside Motel. And she refused to listen to that little voice inside her head that kept trying to tell her it was none of her business, to wait for the complete autopsy results, and to leave it up to the police. By then, she thought, it might be too late. Fonnie didn't clarify to herself what she meant by "too late" or exactly what she meant to do. But she had the whole weekend ahead of her. She might as well start snooping, sniffing, and sleuthing around.

As Fonnie left the dining room, she spotted Hank Peacock in the lobby hunkered deep in a batwing chair. She approached him without hesitation. He was doing a newspaper crossword puzzle and hadn't made much progress. It seemed as good a place as any to start her investigation.

"In my hometown paper," she said, "the Friday puzzles are pretty hard. Is that true in this paper?"

Hank jerked his head up, smiled, laid the paper on his lap. "All crossword puzzles are hard to me. I can't even find a three-letter word for a small salamander."

"Eft. I find puzzle makers like little words that start with e. Like eft, eel, emu, eon."

"You sound like an expert."

"Not really. But I find it a challenge. Nothing like a puzzle to keep the brain circuits running smoothly."

"Or to give one a major case of frustration." He glanced back at the white and black spaces. "Know a word for 'evidence of hard work'? Six letters."

"Sweat comes to mind, but that's only five letters.

I'll get back to you on that one." While she was talking, Fonnie pulled a chair over closer and sat down. She intended to bring the conversation around to the late Buzz Garrison, but she didn't want to sound too abrupt. "Tell me, why are you working on a puzzle if you don't enjoy it?"

"Something to do. And I had to get away from the weeping widow."

"Midge?"

"Yeah. I don't mean to sound uncaring, but she's been crying on Doris's shoulder all afternoon. I was hoping to get home, but Midge doesn't want to leave, and Doris won't go without her. So it looks like we're stuck here."

Fonnie squirmed in her chair, trying to frame her next question. "Was Midge given any details about the autopsy and about why the medical examiner requested a further examination?"

"Not really." Hank stretched, wiggled his hands. "I'm getting stiff sitting around here. Buzz and I had planned on some golf this weekend before heading back to the work-a-day grind. Now I don't know when I'll get back to business."

Fonnie wondered if Hank had avoided her question or if he really didn't know anything about the autopsy. She'd get back to that later. "We didn't have much of a chance to get acquainted before the wedding. What kind of business are you in?"

"I have a Lexus dealership in Richmond. Done pretty good if I do say so myself."

"Is that where you met Paul? He drives a Lexus."

"No. We belong to the same country club, same

civic organizations. Ditto Buzz and Edgar." Hank glanced at the crossword puzzle again and tossed it on the table by his chair. "To heck with that. What I need is a good steak to feed my brain."

"You haven't eaten?"

Hank shook his head. "I was waiting for the gals to come down, but Midge probably can't stop her blubbering long enough to eat."

Fonnie's first reaction to Hank's crude remark was anger, but then she decided the poor man's stomach was doing the talking. Maybe she could maneuver the situation to her own advantage. Her detective instincts told her it would be a good idea to spend some time alone with Midge—time to squeeze out every ounce of information she had. "Call up there, Hank, and tell Doris to come down. I'm sure she needs a break. And tell Midge I'm bringing dinner up to her. That way she'll have a dry shoulder to cry on."

"Great idea." Hank jumped up and dashed for the phone. He turned back and grinned. "I owe you one."

Fonnie started to the dining room to ask for a takeout tray. She turned to Hank, "What room is Midge in now? I heard the desk clerk earlier say he was moving her."

"Two-twenty," Hank said. "Doris helped her move her clothes. They left Buzz's stuff in their old room. I guess it was too much for Midge to handle his things at this point. I'll tell her you'll be up in a little while."

"As soon as I can snag a handsome young waiter. There's no room service here but there's always a way."

THE CLUB WAS JAMMED, the music deafening, the smell overpowering. Keisha had a sneaky suspicion the odor of smoldering pot was co-mingling with sweat and beer. She was relieved, when after a few dances, Stephon suggested they go elsewhere.

"The trouble is, there's not much elsewhere to go." Stephon slid in the car beside her and kept on going. His right arm encircled her shoulders, brought her lips close to his. He kissed her soundly. "Of course, we could move the car to some secluded place and move ourselves to the back seat."

Keisha promptly dislodged his arm, slid over to her door. She smiled sweetly, but her voice was frosty. "I don't do back seats."

Stephon was at a loss for words for about ten seconds. "I hear ya." He turned the key, revved the motor. "And what do you suggest?"

"A booth at McDonald's, a chocolate shake, and conversation."

"Anything you say, ma'am."

Seated at a back booth, Keisha was pensive as she alternated between sipping on her straw and twirling it through the frosty mush. Stephon stirred his shake with a spoon before attempting the straw. "Now about that conversation. Is there something you want to know about me that we haven't already covered?"

"Not exactly. It's just that I was surprised by that remark you made about Midge this afternoon. Practically accusing her of murder. What was behind that?"

"Oh, that? Nothing. My macabre sense of humor. Sometimes it overtakes my good sense."

"Then you don't really believe Midge might have had anything to do with Buzz's death?"

"Naw. But it's true she and Buzz squabbled like alley cats during a full moon."

"What did they squabble about?"

Stephon took a loud slurp before answering. "Anything and everything. Money, bridge scores, weather reports, the federal deficit, NASA. You name it and they could argue about it. It seemed like a game with them." Stephon paused. "Although, at times…."

Keisha stopped mid-sip. "At times, what?"

"I hate to say it, but at times they really seemed mad enough to kill each other."

# ELEVEN

FONNIE KNEW BETTER than to order a heavy meal for Midge. She decided on New England clam chowder, sliced turkey on whole wheat, cheesecake, and hot tea. She gave five dollars to a waiter to deliver the tray.

While Midge's dinner was being prepared, Fonnie went up to her own room. She immediately noted the blinking light on the telephone and hurried to get her message.

"Hi, Gram. Just wanted to touch base with you. I'm calling on my supper break. Melanie filled me in about Buzz's autopsy. I'm sure sending the blood samples and stuff to the state ME is just precautionary. The local ME is probably inexperienced. At any rate, don't be concerned about it. I'm working first shift tomorrow so will call you tomorrow night." There was a slight pause and then Brian added, rather hopefully, Fonnie thought, "Be good and don't get into any trouble."

"Of course, I'll be good," Fonnie said to her mirror image as she gave her silver hair a quick brush back. "It's hard to be bad when I look like Grandma Moses. As soon as I get home, I'm going to have my hair dyed back to red—or maybe pink."

She gave a last swipe with the brush. "But right now

I've got to go comfort a grieving widow and pump her for information."

Fonnie and the waiter appeared at Midge's door at the same time. Fonnie knocked and called in a gentle voice, "Midge, it's me, Fonnie. I've brought you a bite to eat."

A muffled voice answered, "Come on in. It's open."

Midge sniffed, wiped her eyes, and motioned the waiter to set the tray on the table. The young man did as directed and then beat a quick retreat to the door. He paused just long enough to ask if they needed anything else, and seemed relieved when Fonnie shook her head. She sensed that weeping women made him nervous.

Fonnie assumed her "charge nurse" countenance and strode over in front of Midge. "Now, I want you to march yourself to the bathroom, wash your face with cold water, comb your hair, and then come back and eat without sniveling. Do you understand?"

Midge's mouth dropped open and she stared in amazement at Fonnie for a few seconds. Then she nodded her head, gave a tiny smile, got to her feet and aimed for the bathroom.

When she reappeared, Fonnie directed her to a chair in front of the table. "Now eat. Later we'll talk."

Twenty minutes later Midge laid down her napkin by the nearly empty plates. "That was good. I didn't realize I was hungry. Thank you."

"You're welcome. You keep your tea and I'll set the tray in the hallway to be picked up. Then you and I are going to talk."

"About what?"

"First of all tell me exactly what the doctor or the

medical examiner or whoever it was, said when you were notified about the autopsy results."

Midge scrunched up her eyes, sniffed, and reached for the box of tissues. Fonnie beat her to them. "You are not going to cry. You are going to help me find out what happened to Buzz." Fonnie reached over and took Midge's trembling hands. "You owe it to Buzz."

"Yes. Yes, of course. Buzz would want me to be strong." Midge sat up straighter, took a deep breath. "I don't know exactly what was said. Edgar took the call. He'd left a message with the doctor that he was to be notified as my attorney."

"*Is* he your attorney?"

"I guess so. Buzz did all our legal work and now that he's gone…."

"So the medical examiner told Edgar and he told you. Is that right?"

"Yes." Midge sipped her tea and played with her spoon. "All he told me was that they were unable to determine the exact cause of death, and that further tests were indicated—or something like that. He said they were going to send blood samples to the state chief medical examiner." Tears again started streaming down Midge's cheeks. "And the worst thing is they said they might not know anything until after the long weekend."

Fonnie handed Midge back the box of tissues and waited patiently through the mopping up operation. When she thought it was safe to proceed, she asked, "Are you sure Edgar was told Buzz's body could not be released for cremation until they had more information?"

Midge nodded. "I think so. At least, Edgar said he would have to change the arrangements and that he was going to stay here until we knew something definite. So, of course, I'm going to stay also. I can't go home and leave Buzz here."

Fonnie shifted in her chair. "All right. Let's go on to something else—like Florida."

"What do you mean?"

"Tell me about your last few days in Miami. What did you and Buzz do? Who all was there? When did Buzz first get sick? Everything."

"Well, Buzz and I left home—we live south of Richmond—to drive down to Florida the last week of January. We took our time, stopped and visited friends in Raleigh and in Savannah, and got to Miami on the first of February." Midge wrinkled her forehead as if in an effort to remember all the details. "Hank and Doris were already there, been there several days. We've been vacationing together in Miami for years, usually in the late winter. We always stay at the same motel. The boys golf while Doris and I shop. In the evenings we play bridge. Nothing exciting. Just a nice getaway—especially if we're having a cold winter in Virginia. We often run into friends we've made from other years—snowbirds from Michigan and Canada. Edgar and Lula often came down in years past, but not this year. Since Edgar bought this bit of the North Carolina beach, he spends all the time he can here. And of course, Hank's niece, Melanie, lives in Miami and visits when she can get away from the hospital."

"So Melanie visited often?"

"She came over a couple of times that last week. We're a little tame for her tastes though. She likes night life. Last Friday she talked us into going out to a swanky nightclub. I think the boys agreed only because Stephon had dropped in unexpectedly and they didn't know how to entertain him."

Fonnie was getting tired and she began to wonder if this questioning was leading anywhere. It had been a long day and it was warm in the room. Her eyelids began to flutter and she thought longingly of her soft pillow. But when Midge mentioned Stephon, Fonnie's brain sprang back to attention. "Why was Stephon in Miami? Something to do with his real estate job?"

"Oh, no. He came to see a Miami Heat game the next day. I guess he has a friend on the team. At any rate, he knew we were there and dropped in. And it just so happened that Melanie came that same evening and we all ended up going out."

"But Melanie and Stephon didn't know each other before that?" Fonnie felt the answer to this was important, but couldn't explain to herself just why.

"I think they'd met before, when Melanie visited Hank and Doris at their home. They acted like good friends." Midge gave a rueful smile. "Of course, I doubt if Melanie ever met a man who didn't become a good friend. You know what I mean?"

Unfortunately, Fonnie understood exactly what she meant. Poor Brian, she thought. Was he just another number on Melanie's list of conquests?

Before Fonnie's thoughts could wander any further in this direction, Midge went on. "It was the next morning Buzz started getting sick."

"The morning after the nightclub?"

Midge nodded. "I thought he had a hangover. He'd drunk quite a bit that night. Later in the day he felt better. He and Hank played golf in the afternoon. Doris and I went to a dreadful movie. Whoever rated that one G, had to have been blind. When we got back, the boys were having a drink with Stephon. He'd dropped in again, but didn't stay long as he was on his way to the basketball game."

"I see." Fonnie didn't see anything. It was just something to say when one doesn't know *what* to say.

As it happened, she didn't have to say anything else, Midge continued with all the details. "I think Stephon was hoping to run into Melanie again and was disappointed she wasn't there. After he left, Melanie came sweeping in, loaded down with Chinese food. Buzz dug in with gusto. He loves Chinese."

"So he was feeling all right then?"

"Sure was. But then during the night, he started moaning again. Stomach cramps, nausea. I told him I thought he had the flu and he said he thought maybe he'd been drinking too much or maybe getting a stomach ulcer."

"I see." Fonnie let this latest information rattle around in her brain for a few seconds. "And did Stephon return on Sunday?"

"No. He said he was heading home, going to check in at his office and then go to the wedding. And Melanie had told Hank Saturday evening that she wanted to ride up with him and Doris to the wedding. She arranged to work Sunday and Monday and then planned to take a week off. I didn't much like that idea, inviting herself to a wedding just so she could see more of Stephon, but she said it was Stephon's idea."

Midge got up, stretched, went over and looked out

at the darkened skies. She pulled the drapes shut and came back and sat down. "I want to thank you again for getting me off my crying jag. It's done me good to talk. I know I must be boring you."

"No. Not at all. It's very interesting. I like to get a complete picture of things. So you didn't see Melanie Sunday or Monday?"

"No. Tuesday morning Hank and Doris went by her apartment, picked her up, and then we all started up here. Of course, we drove separate cars, but we stayed together. We stopped and had lunch at a delightful little Italian restaurant on the way. Got here in the late afternoon."

"And how was Buzz feeling then?"

"Better, but still queasy. Then the next day he started getting sick again."

"And when did Stephon get here?"

"Wednesday morning. The six of us had lunch together. Then you and Keisha arrived that afternoon." Midge giggled.

"Stephon took one look at Keisha and lost all interest in sweet little Melanie. It's a good thing your grandson arrived when he did or Melanie would have been hard to handle."

"Yes," Fonnie said. "A good thing."

STEPHON WALKED KEISHA to her room, waited while she inserted her card, pushed open the door. She gently blocked his entrance.

"What? You're not inviting me in?"

She shook her head. "Not tonight." She reached up and kissed him lightly on the lips.

He pulled her closer, kissed her deeply. "Goodnight, then. Sleep well."

Fonnie came around the corner just as Keisha backed into her room. She left the door ajar so she could see the encounter between Fonnie and Stephon.

Stephon gave the older woman a big grin. "Evening, Mrs. Beachum."

"Good evening. How was the dance?"

"Crowded. What did you do for entertainment?"

"Listened to Midge tell me all about last weekend in Miami." Keisha noticed Fonnie paused before adding, "It was very interesting."

"Is that so? Well, must be going. Goodnight."

"Goodnight."

Keisha quietly slid her door shut, but not before Fonnie's voice slipped through the crack. "And goodnight to you, too, Keisha."

# TWELVE

SATURDAY STARTED OFF cool and foggy. It matched Fonnie's depressed mood. Last night she'd decided if it wasn't Midge who had poisoned Buzz, then it was either Stephon or Melanie. This morning the fog blurred that notion. After all, she reasoned there were two other people with Buzz all the time: Hank and Doris. Either one could have slipped something into his food or drink over the weekend—not enough to kill him—just enough to make him sick so when the final fatal dose was given, enough to stop his heart, his death wouldn't look all that suspicious.

"Motive," she said in between swipes with her toothbrush. "Who had a motive? What did Hank or Doris have to gain from Buzz's death. Or for that matter—what motive could Melanie and Stephon possibly have? On the surface, it looked like Midge was the only one to gain anything—her freedom from an irritating spouse, life insurance proceeds, perhaps a hefty estate. Fonnie had no idea how well off Buzz was, but she assumed he made fairly good money. But was that enough of a motive?

By the time she finished dressing, Fonnie had almost convinced herself that Buzz's death was natural after all. There had been no poisoning. There was no murderer on the loose. She had been getting herself into a stew over nothing. She'd just been jumping to conclusions. The fog started to lift and Fonnie's mood also lifted as the sun sparkled on the waves.

She brushed her hair in a hurry and hustled down to the dining room. She was hoping to find Jeremiah, to hear what Paul and Amy had said upon hearing the news of Buzz's death, and to discuss the situation with him further.

Jeremiah wasn't in the dining room, but Lula Myers was. She was at a corner table, tapping her fingers and looking angry. Fonnie realized she hadn't seen Lula all day yesterday. She must have kept to her room, Fonnie thought, and wondered now what brought her out so early and why she seemed upset.

She joined Lula on the pretext of hating to eat alone. Lula welcomed her politely and signaled the waitress over. "I'm just having coffee," she said to Fonnie, "but I assume you're a breakfast eater."

"Absolutely. My stomach and my brain both insist on being fed in the morning." Lula smiled and Fonnie thought how pretty she was without her pout. "Sure you won't join me in some blueberry pancakes?"

"No way. It's much too early for my stomach, and my brain is still wondering why I'm out of bed."

The teenage waitress grinned through a tangle of braces, took Fonnie's order and poured Lula more coffee. "Be right back with the best pancakes in the county."

Fonnie started the conversation back. "Then why are you?"

Lula frowned. "Why am I what?"

"Out of bed. You're not looking exactly perky this morning."

"I'm supposed to be taking Melanie to the airport. She asked me last night and I was too drunk to say no. Of course she wasn't in very good shape herself when our goodbye party broke up. I think one of the boys had to help her to her room. Now the men are playing golf and Doris said she was taking Midge to get her hair done this morning so I'm left to tote Melanie around."

Fonnie's brain jumped back a couple of sentences. "Goodbye party? She's going home?"

"Yeah, said there's no excitement around here now—meaning there's no unattached males huffing and puffing at her door."

"So you threw her a party last night?"

"It was Edgar's idea. When she told him she was flying home this morning, he insisted on having the gang up for drinks."

"The gang?" Fonnie was curious to know if Stephon was part of the gang.

"Just Hank, Doris, Tony, and Clara. Edgar called Midge but, as expected, she declined." Lula scowled at her coffee. "Midge is a wet blanket even when she's not in mourning. I hope Edgar isn't going to insist on keeping her in our social circle."

Fonnie's mouth dropped open at the insensitive remark, but Lula didn't seem to notice. She strummed her fingers on the table top. "Melanie better get her tush down here, or she'll be walking back to Miami."

"Maybe she overslept," Fonnie said. "But then I guess you've called her room."

"Called her room, her cell phone, had her paged. Nothing."

"Maybe she took a run on the beach and forgot the time."

Fonnie's pancakes arrived and she busied herself covering them with butter and syrup.

Lula finished her coffee and stood up. "You'll have to excuse me, but I'm not waiting any longer. If you see her, tell Melanie I've gone back to bed and she'll have to call a taxi."

Jeremiah came up a minute after Lula left and plopped down across from Fonnie. She swiped at a drop of syrup dribbling down her chin. He was dressed in a sky-blue sweat suit and smelled of musk. Fonnie inhaled deeply, gave him a welcoming smile. "I guess you're ready for your mid-morning snack by now."

"That's right. Been up for hours. Been wanting to talk to you."

"I'm flattered. Or shouldn't I be? Is this business rather than pleasure?"

"Both. Talked to Paul and Amy last night. They wanted to fly in this afternoon."

"But there's no need," Fonnie said.

"Told them that. And they finally agreed. They're coming back Wednesday as they had originally planned." Jeremiah waved to the passing waitress and she nodded. "When I told Paul about the autopsy and all, he said something rather strange."

"Strange? What do you mean? What did he say?"

"He said, 'I knew Buzz was worried. I should have talked to him about it.'"

The young waitress came up and Jeremiah ordered

coffee and an English muffin. He then turned back to Fonnie. "You reckon something's going on in that law firm that isn't quite kosher?" Before Fonnie could respond, Jeremiah went on, "And there's another odd thing."

"What's that?" Fonnie asked.

"Tony. Clara said he was anxious to get home today, but now he's changed his mind. He thinks they ought to stay since Midge is staying and she's so upset."

"Was Tony that close to Buzz and Midge?"

"I didn't think so. He managed some of Buzz's investments, played golf with him, but I didn't think it went any further than that. Anyway, Clara says they're going to stay over the long weekend."

"Actually, I'm glad about that. It'll give me a chance to get better acquainted with Clara."

Keisha was sitting up in bed enjoying her second cup of coffee. Thank goodness for the coffee maker in the room. She hated getting dressed immediately upon awakening. This way she could mull over last evening and the coming day without having to make small talk with anybody.

Okay, what about last evening? She hadn't jumped out of bed this morning singing love songs as she had yesterday. She was fond of Stephon—very fond of him, but were things moving too fast? Did she really know him? And had Fonnie started acting rather distant to him? What was that all about?

And today? Stephon had suggested they take a picnic lunch and spend the day exploring beaches and possibly a lighthouse. She had murmured something about spending some time with Fonnie that seemed to irritate him. She stared out at the fog and was rather hoping it would last all day. Maybe that would automatically rule out a picnic. She had heard Fonnie leave her room a little earlier, and decided to try to join up with her in a little bit.

The phone by her bed rang. She picked it up slowly, trying to figure out what she was going to say to Stephon. But the first sound of his laughing voice erased all doubts from her mind. Of course she wanted to spend the day with him. Of course the fog would soon lift and they could enjoy a picnic on the beach, climb a lighthouse, maybe even fly to the moon.

They agreed to meet under the pier behind the motel. He would get the picnic stuff and she would make her excuses to Fonnie. It was going to be a glorious day.

The weather *was* beautiful, one of those rare perfect days that southern Februarys toss in between frigid winds and snow flurries and downpours. The thermometer stretched into the sixties and the sun shone like a benevolent god.

The picnickers finished the last chicken salad sandwich, the last chocolate-chip cookie, slurped the last of the iced tea.

The quilt Stephon had dragged out of his car covered the bit of the beach they claimed for their own. Lying on their backs, they studied the whimsical clouds, told their family histories, whispered their dreams, locked their fingers. Somewhere along the way, their voices faded, their eyes closed, they napped.

Keisha was awakened by a plop of dampness on her cheek. The sun had disappeared, the temperature had dropped, and it had started to sprinkle.

By the time they got back to the car, they were soaked. "So much for the perfect day," Stephon growled as he tossed the quilt in the back seat.

Keisha swiped her hair back out of her eyes and laughed. "Like my daddy, the preacher, says, 'Into each life some rain must fall.'"

Stephon smiled, took her hand. "Think your daddy will like me?"

"Probably not. But I do. That's all that matters."

FONNIE AND JEREMIAH also took advantage of the lovely morning. Instead of the beach, though, they wandered in and out of antique shops, laughed when they found artifacts that were common in their childhood and sighed over an exhibit of quaint valentines. They had lunch at a replica of an old-fashioned ice cream parlor.

Jeremiah noted the dark clouds approaching from the east and they made it back to the motel before the rain set in. They walked into the lobby and straight into the middle of an argument.

Edgar had his hands on his hips and was glaring at Lula. "But you agreed to take her to the airport."

Lula tossed her head. "Could I help it if the dingbat didn't show? I was up waiting for her." Lula grabbed Fonnie by the hand. "Just ask Fonnie if you don't believe me. She was with me at that ungodly hour." She turned to Fonnie. "Tell him. Wasn't I waiting for Melanie?"

Fonnie looked around in puzzlement. "Sure. You were looking for her. What's the matter? Did she miss her plane?"

Hank nodded his head, his face a mask of worry.

"She missed her plane all right, but the worst of it is that *she's* missing!"

Jeremiah shoved forward. "What do you mean, missing?"

"I mean missing. She's not here. She's nowhere around." Hank clenched his fists. "My niece is missing."

"Now just calm down," Jeremiah said. "How do you know she's missing?"

"When Lula told me she hadn't taken Melanie to the airport, I called the airline. She wasn't on her booked flight or any other flight. The desk clerk said she hadn't checked out of her room, but there was no answer to my knock. That's when I really started getting worried. I called Edgar and he told the desk clerk to let me into her room. Her bed hadn't been slept in. Her things are all still there, even her purse. But she's gone—disappeared."

# THIRTEEN

WHEN HANK DECLARED that Melanie had disappeared, Fonnie studied the people around her. Edgar was glaring at Lula, Lula looked disgusted, Doris was sniffling, Tony was pacing, Clara was staring at Tony.

"You called the police?" Jeremiah asked.

"Of course, I called the police," Hank nearly screamed. "The gal that took my call muttered something about twenty-four hours, but said she would pass the word along and maybe someone would be out to investigate." He threw his hands up. "Can you believe that? *Maybe* someone from the police would come out."

It was at this juncture Keisha and Stephon came in. Fonnie tried to explain the commotion while at the same time telling them they should go to their rooms and get on some dry clothes.

Stephon wiped his hand across his face. "Melanie missing? I'm sure she'll turn up somewhere. She seemed fine last night."

"You saw her last night?" Keisha's voice held a definite edge.

"Yeah. When Tony took her to her room. Her room is next door to mine. I'd gone to get some ice after I said goodnight to you. I waved to both of them as they went in. I don't know if they saw me or not."

All eyes rotated to Tony. His face paled. Hank came up closer. "You went to her room? And where was Clara while this was going on?"

"Hey!" Tony said. "You've got it all wrong. Remember Clara had a headache and left the party early. I was getting ready to leave after you and Doris did. Melanie looked a little unsteady on her feet. So I saw her to her room to be sure she got there all right."

"But you went in?" Hank was now nearly in Tony's face.

"Just for a second. Just to be sure she was okay." Tony backed away from Hank and appealed to Stephon. "You saw me leave her room, didn't you? I wasn't in there but a minute."

Stephon shook his head. "Sorry, I went on into my room. I didn't see or hear anything else."

Edgar, who had been listening carefully, came up and slapped Hank on the back. "I think we all need to calm down. There's got to be a logical explanation. It must be that Melanie decided to go back out after Tony left her. She may have met someone else, had more to drink, and passed out." He laughed. "Some poor slob is probably waking up right now and wondering how that beautiful blonde got into his bed. She'll be crawling out of a hole somewhere soon and not a bit worse for wear."

So that's the reputation Melanie has, Fonnie thought. She was glad Brian wasn't around to hear it.

"I really have to get out of these wet clothes," Keisha whispered to Fonnie.

Fonnie nodded. "I'm going up in a little bit. Come to my room when you get changed and we'll talk."

Keisha shed her clothes and jumped into the shower. She was chilled in both her body and her mind. The hot water stilled her shivering, but her brain was still disturbed. Poor Melanie, she thought. Keisha hadn't much liked the girl, but she hoped nothing bad had happened to her. And just for a second, a disturbing thought fluttered through her mind. Maybe Melanie had seen Stephon waving at her and had taken it as an invitation. What would Stephon had done if Melanie had come knocking at his door? Nonsense. He would have mentioned it if that had happened and he certainly wouldn't have invited Melanie in.

Keisha kept pondering Melanie's possible whereabouts as she dried off and slipped into warm slacks and a sweater.

FONNIE ANXIOUSLY waited for Keisha. She was worried about her young friend. Was Keisha being taken for a romantic ride by Stephon as Brian had been by Melanie? Fonnie hated to admit it to herself, but she had misjudged Melanie big time. Now she was having ambivalent feelings about Stephon. On the surface he seemed like a nice young man. Amy liked him and Keisha was obviously infatuated. But Fonnie had some qualms about him. Had he told Keisha about being in Miami, about being with Melanie? And after he had waved goodnight to Melanie, had he really gone into his room and not come back out? What if he had waited for Tony to leave Melanie's room and then paid her a visit? Or was there a connecting door between his room and hers that could be opened by mutual consent? So many questions with no answers.

There was a faint knock on the door. Almost timid. But, Fonnie thought, Keisha was never timid. She slowly opened the door.

It was Doris. "So sorry to intrude. But I'd like to talk to you if you don't mind."

"Of course, I don't mind. Do come in." Fonnie motioned Doris to a chair. "What can I do for you?"

Doris grimaced. "Nothing, actually. I'm just upset and I need an understanding ear."

"I can understand why you're upset about Melanie being missing. It must be hard."

"It's not that—not really. It's that I had talked Midge into going home in the morning. She agreed to let me drive her car while Hank drove ours. I was so looking forward to getting out of here and back home again. Now Melanie's messed that plan up. Hank won't leave until she's found and I'm stuck here."

"But you're not worried about Melanie?"

"Nah. I think she found someone to shack up with. She doesn't give a damn about worrying other people. She never has."

Another knock on the door, this time firm and loud, saved Fonnie from continuing the depressing conversation. "That must be Keisha." Fonnie hurried to open the door. She grabbed Keisha and gave her a quick hug before ushering her in. Keisha gave Fonnie a strange look, but Fonnie just grinned. It was hard to explain, even to herself, but Fonnie felt like a breath of fresh air had just entered the room.

"Stephon called from the lobby," Keisha said. "Two policemen showed up. They're going to start searching the grounds after they check out Melanie's room.

It's not officially a missing person case yet, but they agree it's odd, that if she went off on her own, she didn't even take her purse."

"Oh, dear," Doris said. "I didn't think about that. Maybe she really did meet with foul play. I'd better get back to Hank. He'll be going crazy. And Midge. What am I going to tell Midge? Oh, dear. Oh, dear."

Keisha opened the door for Doris. "Let me know if there's anything I can do." Doris nodded and sped toward the elevator.

Fonnie flopped down in the chair Doris had vacated. "What a nightmare. Buzz dead. Melanie missing. I feel like I'm in an episode of *Unsolved Mysteries*."

Keisha walked to the window, stared out at the drizzling rain. The storm had passed quickly and the sun was trying to peek through the remaining clouds. There was sadness in her voice when she spoke. "I'm sure there's a solution, but I'm afraid when we find the answer, we're not going to like it."

The afternoon was spent in searching. Fonnie overheard Edgar assign a maid to look into every unoccupied room, and she watched as the policemen knocked on the other doors. The policemen explained about a young woman being missing, gave her description and asked if the occupants had seen anybody resembling her. Apparently no one had.

After the rain stopped, the policemen and Melanie's friends scattered outside. They went over the motel grounds, the beach area, the parking lot, even peered into the parked cars.

Fonnie heard one of the policemen say he was going back inside and check all the storage areas and linen closets. She followed him in and was in the lobby when he met up with another uniformed policeman. Fonnie was close enough to hear their conversation.

"Nothing?" one of them asked the other.

"Nothing. She's vanished. And I don't think it was of her own free will."

"What do you make of the stories of the two guys who supposedly saw her last?" He checked his notebook. "Tony Cauthen and Stephon Weber. Are they telling it straight?"

"Hard to tell and we can't push them yet. I did notice that the connecting door between Weber's room and that of the missing girl was locked from her side—if that means anything. But if the gal doesn't show by morning, then we've got ourselves a case, and we'll go after them."

# FOURTEEN

A DISPIRITED GROUP gathered for a late dinner. Fonnie, Jeremiah, Stephon, and Keisha sat at one table. Hank, Doris, Midge, Clara, and Tony were at another. Edgar had told them he and Lula were having dinner sent up to their suite.

Although Lula had joined in the search for a while that afternoon, when it came close to five o'clock, she made an excuse to leave, and Fonnie feared that by now Lula may have already drunk most of her dinner. Fonnie liked Lula but wondered what demons tormented her.

Silence hovered over the two tables. Everything that could be said about the missing woman had been said several times over. And it didn't seem fitting to bring up any other subject.

But Fonnie's mind kept going back over the conversations she'd had with different people. Clara had told her she didn't know what time Tony had come to bed. She'd taken pain medication for her headache and was asleep when he came in. Hank insisted that Melanie had not drunk very much and was fine when he and Doris left the party. Stephon's room was next to Melanie's but he said he didn't hear Tony leave. Edgar said he went right to bed after everybody left and that

Lula was already sleeping. Midge hadn't gone to the party and said Melanie had stopped in to say goodbye before she went up to Edgar and Lula's suite.

At one point in the afternoon, when Fonnie and Keisha sat resting on the verandah, Midge joined them and seemed anxious to talk about the missing girl. As she nibbled at her salad, Fonnie replayed the conversation over in her mind. Midge had started off by saying, "I admit I didn't always like Melanie, but she could be sweet. And Buzz thought a lot of her."

"Oh, she could be a real charmer," Keisha said as she gave her rocker an extra shove.

Fonnie detected the sarcasm in Keisha's voice, but apparently Midge didn't. "That she could," Midge said. "And you know, for all her sophistication, she had her childlike qualities."

Keisha stopped rocking and asked, "Like what?"

"Like her funky jewelry. She wore that silly charm bracelet most all the time, even at the wedding. You must have noticed it. It had all the signs of the zodiac on it: a bull, a lion, a fish, and all the rest. She especially liked the scorpion because that represented her birthday. She had it on last night when she came to see me, and that silly lip-gloss ring too."

Fonnie turned her head to stare at Midge. "Lip-gloss ring? What on earth is that?"

"It looks like a regular ring, sterling silver, but it opens up and there's lip gloss inside. So after you eat or drink something, you can flip it open, get a little on a finger and rub it over your lips. Instant beauty."

Keisha laughed. "I noticed she wore that at the wedding reception, but I didn't see her use it. I guess she was too wrapped up in Brian to worry about whether her lips were glossy or not."

"I can understand her love of flashy jewelry," Fonnie said. "A nurse can't wear much jewelry while working, so she may go way out when off duty. I love chunky necklaces myself." Fonnie brought herself back to the present by fingering the simple pearls around her neck. "And I'm going back to wearing them as soon as I get home."

Chairs began to scrape away from the tables. People started saying goodnight and headed toward their rooms. There would be no partying tonight.

"Sleep well, Fonnie," Jeremiah said. "Try not to worry. I'll see you in the morning."

Fonnie nodded. Keisha and Stephon were already in the lobby. They looked her way. Stephon gave Keisha a quick kiss on the cheek and hurried to the elevator. Keisha waited for Fonnie, and they took the next elevator to their floor. They smiled goodnight as there seemed nothing else to say.

Fonnie closed and locked her door. She pulled the drapes tight over the windows, wishing she could block out everything that had happened this afternoon.

She was crawling into bed before she noticed the red light blinking on her phone. "Brian." Her hand flew to her mouth. "What am I going to tell him?"

She pushed the button for the message. Brian's cheery voice seemed so out of place in the gloomy room. "Hey, Gram. Just checking on you. Melanie called me last night and said she was going home today. She gave me her home number, but I can't get an answer there. Guess I'll have to try tomorrow. When are you and Keisha coming home? I miss you. Bye."

As much as she hated to, Fonnie knew she had to call him back. He answered on the first ring. She could tell he had his mouth full. "Hmm. Hey."

"Hey yourself." Fonnie tried to keep her tone light, but it was no use. Her voice broke as soon as she started talking. She told Brian about Melanie's disappearance, the search, the uncertainty.

Brian seemed stunned. When she finished, he said very quietly. "I'm going to call the police station there. Maybe they can give me some more info. Maybe it's not as bad as it sounds." He caught his breath.

Fonnie could tell he was trying hard to maintain his composure. Her heart went out to him. There was no way she was going to tell him now what she had learned of Melanie's reputation. "Call me in the morning," she said. "Maybe we'll know more then."

MORNING BROUGHT ONLY more mystery, more blank looks, more police. It also brought a detective, Lieutenant Max Steinberg, who strolled into the dining room, found Fonnie's table and introduced himself. The same quartet who had shared a table the evening before was again together: Fonnie, Keisha, Jeremiah, and Stephon.

Fonnie studied the man as he gave his name, rank, and the reason for his visit. He was dressed in a gray business suit, fiftyish, tall, muscular, and sported a thin dark mustache which he massaged as he looked around the table. Fonnie wondered if the mustache was new, maybe in compensation for the thinning hair on top of his head.

"Sorry to interrupt breakfast," he said to the group

in general, "but since there's been no news of the subject and it's been over twenty-four hours, we now have an official missing person case on our hands. We best get started with investigating." He pulled up a chair and his eyes focused on Fonnie. "Mrs. Beachum?"

Fonnie peered at him over the rim of her coffee cup, took a slow sip, and then answered, "Yes." She set the cup down, gave him a quizzical look. "How do you know my name?"

"Your grandson described you."

Fonnie grinned, sat up straighter. "You talked to Brian? He said he was going to call the police station, but I didn't know he was going to cut to the top brass."

Max Steinberg pulled up a chair from an empty table, sat down, and returned her grin. "I'm not exactly top-brass, and Officer Hendley warned me about you trying to smooth-talk your way into getting confidential information."

"Me? Smooth-talk?" Fonnie gave him what she considered an innocent gaze. "Whatever did Brian mean?"

"I suspect I'll find out. But right now, I want each of you to tell me again your recollection of the last time you saw Melanie Peacock and anything you think may be pertinent to the case."

Keisha turned worried eyes to the detective. "Do you think something terrible has happened to Melanie?"

"I don't think she went for a walk and got lost. What do you think happened?"

"I don't know." She wrapped her arms tightly around herself and gave a slight shudder. "I don't even want to imagine."

Steinberg shook his head. "Neither do I." He pushed

back his chair, rose to his feet. “I want to talk to each of you separately. The motel has set us up in the office behind the desk.” He pulled a paper from his pocket, glanced at the names. “I’ll start with Stephon Weber.”

Stephon jerked his head. “Me?”

“Yes sir. You can come with me now.” He turned back to the others. “I’ll get up with the rest of you later. If you don’t mind, I’d appreciate you staying around here or in the lobby. Then if you want, you can join the search.”

Jeremiah spoke up, “The search?”

“We’re going to search every inch of the beach and surrounding buildings today. I know the area was searched yesterday, but it was cursory. Today we’re going to do it right. Since it’s Sunday, I’m sending officers to every church in the county to solicit help from our fine citizens. If Miss Peacock is anywhere in the open, we’ll find her.”

“And if she’s stuffed in someone’s closet,” Jeremiah said. “What then?”

“It’ll take a little longer.”

Steinberg wiggled a finger at Stephon and the two of them left the dining room.

Keisha watched them walk away. She shook her head. “I don’t understand. Why does he want to talk to Stephon? He didn’t see Melanie after Tony took her to her room.” She looked from Fonnie to Jeremiah and back again. “What could he possibly know?”

Jeremiah shrugged. “What do any of us know? The police have to go over everyone’s story again. They’re just doing their job.” He swivelled his head around to Fonnie. “Right?”

Fonnie hesitated. Her mind went back to Keisha's last statement. Had Stephon seen Melanie again? Surely not. But it still bothered her that he hadn't told Keisha about having known Melanie previously, about having been in Miami the weekend before the wedding. Maybe now was the time to tell her.

Jeremiah waved his hand in front of Fonnie's face. "Earth to Fonnie. Come in Fonnie, from whatever galaxy you're in."

Fonnie blinked. "I'm sorry. My mind got side-tracked." She took a deep breath, reached over and touched Keisha's arm. "There's something I have to tell you. It may be upsetting, but hear me out."

"Tell me what? You sound so mysterious."

Jeremiah finished his coffee with a loud slurp. "Want me to leave?"

"No. I want you to hear it also and give us your opinion."

Fonnie proceeded to tell Keisha and Jeremiah about Midge's account of Stephon's visit to Miami. Keisha listened in silence, her facial expression seemed to change from perplexity to disbelief and finally to fury.

But to Fonnie's surprise, the fury was against Midge, not Stephon. "So what if Stephon was in Miami? It's a free country. He can go where he wants. Midge just wants to get him in trouble. Implying that there was something between him and Melanie, that he may have had something to do with her disappearance."

Jeremiah frowned. "I don't think you're getting the picture, Keisha. Midge told Fonnie this story before Melanie disappeared. She was telling it in reference to the possible poisoning of Buzz. Stephon was there when Buzz first got sick."

Tears seeped into Keisha's eyes. She tried to blink them back. She stared at Fonnie. "I thought you liked Stephon. Now you've turned against him. Accusing him of murder and of kidnapping. What next? Are you going to tell me he's a serial killer?"

"No, no, no." Fonnie shook her head with a frantic motion. "I'm not accusing him of anything. I'm simply saying that he didn't seem to be up-front with you about his relationship with Melanie. Did he ever mention to you about knowing her previously?"

Keisha bent her head toward the table. She grabbed her napkin and swiped the tears from her cheeks. When she lifted her head, her eyes were belligerent. "No. But then I didn't ask him. If I had asked him, he would have told me. It's not that he lied to me."

"Perhaps not. But it strikes me that it may fall into that gray area known as sins of omission." Fonnie knew she had to tell Keisha one more fact and this was going to be even harder. She braced herself for Keisha's anger. "Melanie told me herself," Fonnie went on, "that she came to the wedding just so she could spend more time with Stephon, and that he had suggested it."

"That's a lie! Melanie said that just to make me jealous."

"That hardly seems likely," Jeremiah said. "If that had been the case, she would have told you directly. But she didn't tell you. She mentioned it offhand to Fonnie. By then, she and Brian had become a twosome, and so Stephon didn't matter to her any further."

Jeremiah tapped his spoon against the table a few times, then looked up and smiled at Keisha. "But I think I can understand why Stephon didn't say anything to you about knowing Melanie." Both Keisha and Fonnie turned their complete attention to him. "It's really very simple," he said. "After all, he'd just met a beautiful and charming girl and probably fell for her immediately. In cases like that, a man doesn't mention any other girls he knows or has dated. That might squash the romance before it had a chance to get started. He couldn't risk that."

Keisha's smile broke out like the sun coming from behind a cloud. "Yes, that must be the reason. And he would have told me when the time was right. He just didn't want to spoil our friendship with something that didn't really matter." She leaned back in her chair. "Thank you, Jeremiah. I feel so much better."

Fonnie kicked Jeremiah's ankle under the table at the same time she beamed at Keisha. "Now why didn't I think of that?"

"Because you've let all the romance go out of your life," Jeremiah said. "A situation I intend to remedy as soon as all this other mess is cleaned up."

Keisha laughed. "That I've got to see. But right now I'm going to see about my own romance. The detective should be through quizzing Stephon by now. Maybe I can be next in line and then Stephon and I can join the searchers." She got up, bent over and kissed Jeremiah on the cheek. "Thanks again."

When Keisha was out of hearing range, Fonnie let Jeremiah have it. She slapped the table with her right hand and stuck her face close to his. "Lost my romance, have I? What you've lost is your common sense. You don't for one instant believe that rubbish you fed Keisha. You were just trying to make her feel good."

"And what was wrong with that? That poor gal needed a life preserver and that's what I threw to her. If the truth is any different, she'll find out in her own time and she'll handle it in her own way. And when that time comes, you need to be there for her. Not to say, 'I told you so,' but as a friend, to help pick up the pieces."

Fonnie dropped her head. "You're right, of course. Sometimes I get a little carried away with facts and forget about feelings. It won't happen again."

"Sure it will. But that's okay. You stick to getting all the facts and I'll follow you around and sooth the ruffled feelings you leave in your wake. I think we'll make a pretty good team of detectives."

"That we will."

# FIFTEEN

FONNIE SAT IN THE LOBBY and watched as people trooped in and out of the detective's temporary office. She studied their faces. Some were blank, some looked nervous, some seemed aggravated. She wished she could have been privy to their conversations. She wondered what tidbits they would reveal to Lieutenant Steinberg that she hadn't been able to worm out of them earlier.

Finally it was Fonnie's turn. It didn't take long for her to tell her story to Lieutenant Steinberg. She told him she'd last seen Melanie on Friday evening in the dining room. "She'd come in from a run on the beach and had a cup of coffee with me. We talked some." Fonnie paused.

The detective waited, rubbed his mustache, shifted in his chair. Finally Fonnie went on. "I might as well tell you, I got angry with her and left in rather a huff."

"Really? So suppose you tell me what you talked about and what made you angry?"

"We talked about the Buzz Garrison case." Fonnie propped her right elbow on the desk between them and leaned forward. "You are aware of his suspicious death, aren't you?"

Steinberg's lips curved slightly upward. "I'm aware

of the unexpected death. I wasn't aware that it had become a police case."

"Well, maybe it hasn't yet, but it will. Mark my words. The man was poisoned. Why else would they be sending blood and tissue samples to the state medical examiner?

"I see. And you think that indicates the ME suspects poisoning?"

"Definitely. Of course, it could turn out to be food poisoning, something he picked up in Florida. Could even be accidental." Fonnie leaned back in her chair. "But I have my ideas, and I'm willing to share them with you. I may be of help in the case, if in turn, you'll share what you know with me."

This time there was no mistaking the detective's amused smile. "I think I'm beginning to understand what your grandson meant about smooth-talking me."

"In that case, I'll forget the smooth-talking and get right to the point. I think Melanie's disappearance is connected to Buzz's death. She kept saying she thought his death was simply a heart attack. But what if she found out something that belied that conviction? Maybe she remembered some symptom, a suspicious action on someone's part, maybe Buzz said something in the ambulance. Melanie learned something that was dangerous to the killer. So she had to be removed too. Is that pretty much in line with your thinking?"

Steinberg's smile died on his lips. "Mrs. Beachum, let's get back to me asking the questions and you answering. Suppose first you tell me what Miss Peacock said to you Friday night that made you angry."

Fonnie nodded. "Sure. We'll play the game your

way. So, to answer your question, Melanie hinted that my new son-in-law, Paul Trent, may have benefited from Buzz Garrison's death."

"And how would that be?"

"By rising in the law firm to a more prominent position. Actually, that's probably true, but her insinuation that Paul may have been responsible for the death was slanderous. And it made me mad."

"Yes, I can understand that. Did the conversation end there?"

"No. Melanie then apologized for upsetting me and said she'd only been joking. But I got to thinking later on. What if she had joked with someone else about poisoning Buzz? She may have found out or imagined how a certain person benefited from his death and made a joke about it. But maybe she hit too close to home, and that certain person had to eliminate her also."

"So you think Melanie Peacock has been eliminated?"

"Yes. Don't you?"

The detective rose to his feet and opened the door. "That'll be all for now, Mrs. Beachum. I'll let you know if you can be of any further help."

Fonnie reluctantly left the office, wandered out to the motel verandah, dropped down in a reclining chair. She wanted to join in the search, but her legs remained too wobbly. All the excitement of the past days had gotten to her. Although she'd made great strides in recovering from her stroke, she still had limitations. All she could do right now was rest and pray.

She could see Keisha and Stephon walking toward the marina. They were in a group getting directions from a uniformed officer. Earlier she had overheard two policemen talking, and they mentioned having a search warrant for all of the motel rooms. Maybe they had one to search the boats, also. Fonnie's brain vacillated between wanting the searchers to find their objective and not wanting them to. If they find something, she reasoned, it will be a dead body. If they don't find Melanie, then there remained the hope, faint as it might be, that she was still alive.

Fonnie thought over the comments she'd overheard in the lobby while waiting to be called in by the detective. The speculations of strangers who had come to help ranged from a sex maniac on the prowl, to a kidnapping for ransom, to a terrorist plot. But Fonnie had no doubt she was right when she insisted Melanie's disappearance was linked to Buzz's death.

The search went on all day. People straggled in for lunch and for short respites, then moved out again. Fonnie saw Red Cross volunteers distributing sandwiches and cold drinks.

Occasionally she glimpsed Max Steinberg conferring with his men or with Edgar. As owner of the motel, she realized Edgar must be going through a very difficult time. Could he be held liable for inadequate security if someone had forced his way into Melanie's room?

Earlier in the day Fonnie had seen Hank, Doris, and Midge in a group following an officer to the northern end of the beach. Clara and Tony ventured off in the opposite direction.

Jeremiah came in about mid-afternoon. He had nothing to report and nothing to say. He collapsed in a chair next to Fonnie, reached over and squeezed her hand. She understood. There was nothing anybody could say at this point.

Near dark the search was called off. Edgar had instructed the kitchen crew to set up a free buffet on the verandah. Weary searchers filled Styrofoam plates, downed gallons of coffee, whispered in small groups.

Keisha and Stephon were among the last of the searchers to return to the motel. They trudged up the steps hand in hand, but there was nothing romantic in their mood. They both looked like they had been through a war. Fonnie hadn't intended to eat, but she knew Keisha had to have some nourishment. "Set yourself down here, child, while I fix us some plates. I was waiting until I had some good company to eat with."

Keisha shook her head. "I'm afraid I'm not good company tonight. You go ahead. I'll just have some coffee."

"Nonsense. Both you and Stephon look like you're about to drop. Come on, Stephon, help me load up some food."

"Sure," Stephon said, "why not? I ought to be able to take a few more steps."

After potato salad, baked beans, and fried chicken they all felt better. Stephon even went back for a piece of apple pie. Fonnie and Keisha declined dessert.

"You take your time," Keisha said to Stephon, "I'm going to see Fonnie to her room and then I'm going to pass out." She bent over and kissed him on the cheek. "See you in the morning."

As they passed the desk, Fonnie noticed a Trailways bus pulled up by the door, and the bus driver leaning over the desk.

"I don't know as I can accommodate all of you," the desk clerk said. "I'll see what I can do. Some of the ladies may have to double up."

"That'll be fine. We were supposed to make it to Wilmington tonight, but we had a little engine trouble on the way. Appreciate you making room for us."

Fonnie and Keisha caught the next elevator up. "That bus driver looked whipped," Fonnie said. "Poor fellow. I hope there's enough rooms for his passengers."

Keisha nodded. "I'm sure there will be, but don't you start worrying about them. It's not your problem. I'll stop by and get you for breakfast."

Fonnie wanted nothing more than to crawl into bed and lapse into neverland, but she had to do one more thing before calling it a day. She dialed her home phone and spent the next several minutes filling Brian in on the results, or rather the non-results, of the search for Melanie. He knew most of it already since he'd been in contact with the police department here. What Fonnie didn't tell her grandson was what she'd learned about Melanie's reputation. If he found that out, it would have to be from some other source. She promised to call him tomorrow night with any further news.

"I'm starting second shift tomorrow," Brian said. "Call me about noon if you get a chance. I can keep in touch with their department while I'm working, so I won't miss anything. And Gram, don't give the police there any grief."

Any other time a remark like that would have gotten her dander up, but tonight Fonnie was too tired to respond. She told him goodnight and fell into bed.

# SIXTEEN

KEISHA FLOPPED DOWN on her bed without undressing. She lay there a long time, her mind a whirlwind. She knew Stephon had wanted her to invite him to her room. But she didn't want to. She needed time alone, time to think.

The ringing phone startled her. Oh, no, she thought, what does Stephon want now? But it wasn't Stephon.

"Keisha, Doris here. I know it's late but I hope I caught you before you got to bed."

"No, I'm not in bed. Can I do something for you?"

"Yes. I know it's cheeky of me to ask, but I need some help. It probably wouldn't take but a few minutes."

"Certainly. What is it?"

"The desk clerk just called up and asked Midge to remove the rest of her stuff from the room she and Buzz had. He said a busload of tourists just drove up and they need the room. Actually, I thought the clerk had a lot of gall. Edgar had said just to leave Buzz's stuff in there and that he'd take care of it himself. The clerk said he'd checked with Edgar and that the room did have to be vacated. I can't get hold of Edgar now and Midge is upset. Since you're right across the hall, I thought maybe you wouldn't mind going over there and packing up everything. Midge still has the key card and I could bring it up."

Keisha hesitated. "Well—sure. I could do that. I'd be glad to do it. And I'll just keep their suitcases in my room until she's ready to go home or whatever."

"Oh, thank you. Midge will be so relieved."

Keisha got off the bed, went to the bathroom and splashed some cold water on her face. "Will this day never end?"

In a short while Doris tapped on the door and handed Keisha the key card. "Just let the desk clerk know when you're done. Thanks again." Doris waved a tiny goodbye and disappeared down the hall.

"Sure," Keisha said to Doris's back. Leaving the door open, she jammed her own card into her pocket, took the one Doris had given her, and was about to leave the room when the phone rang again. "Now what?"

She grabbed the phone and tried not to sound unpleasant. "Yes?"

This time it was Stephon. "No," she answered after she heard his plea. "You can't come up and I can't come down to your room even if I wanted to. I've got to do a favor for Midge. The desk clerk insists the room Buzz was in be vacated. Since it's right across the hall from me, I'm going to pack his clothes and stuff." She let out a deep sigh. "And then I'm going to bed. Don't be mad, but I'm bushed. See you in the morning. Night-night."

Keisha shut her door tightly, crossed the hall, and opened that door.

"Jeez," she said out loud. "What a mess. Midge didn't waste any time straightening up when she packed her own things. She must have left it this way. Or maybe the police left the clutter when they searched the room today." The closet door stood open. Pants, shirts, jackets hung every which way, some halfway off their hangers, some on the floor. Socks and underwear spilled out of an open dresser drawer. "No wonder Midge didn't want to come back in here."

Keisha left the door to the room open a few inches. For some reason she didn't want to be shut up with the belongings of a dead man. She hauled a large suitcase out of the closet and started packing. She emptied the drawers first, folding shorts and undershirts neatly, placing pairs of socks around the edges. In a smaller bag she placed everything left in the bathroom: shampoo, deodorant, electric razor, toothbrush, nail clippers. Men are so lucky, Keisha thought, they only need the bare essentials to survive.

She saved the closet for last. She carefully hand-pressed the pants and laid them flat, followed by a half-dozen shirts. Then the thought came to her that she ought to check the pockets. After all, these clothes would probably be donated to some charity and Keisha was sure Midge wouldn't bother to go through them.

So Keisha took the pants out and dug into each pocket. She found only two movie ticket stubs, a golf tee, a half roll of Tums, and sixty eight cents in change. In one shirt pocket was a gas receipt and in another was a lottery ticket. She dumped everything in with the razor and toothbrush. Then she started with the coats and jackets. Just more of the same—minutiae of daily life.

She was about to do the final fold of a light rain jacket when her fingers felt an inside zipper. She opened the jacket wide, zipped down the zipper, and explored the recess. Her fingers found a partially folded piece of white paper. The letterhead was visible:

Myers, Garrison, and Trent Law Firm. Keisha was about to toss it on top of the razor when she noticed a scribbled note in red ink next to some figures. She read the words, "consulting fees???" It was the question marks that intrigued her.

She sat down on the side of the bed and spread the paper open. She wasn't sure what she was looking at. An audit? An internal report? It wasn't addressed to anyone nor was it signed. It consisted of various names, perhaps of companies, followed by numbers. Comments and questions scribbled in red spread across the report. It was apparent Buzz, or whoever had wielded the red pen, had jotted down ideas as they came to him in no particular order. Keisha assumed these were items or ideas that puzzled him because of the numerous question marks scattered around. Next to the name, "Klondike Foundation," was written, "how?" Below this was, "why??"

Another entry read "Trentstone" followed by more question marks. Keisha was sure she'd heard that name before. She turned the name around and around in her head and finally the answer came to her. Stephon had mentioned that Trentstone Estates was a new upscale housing development that Amy was involved in. Had Buzz suspected something crooked about it?

All of the writing was hurried, hard to read, and many words seemed pure legalese. Keisha was able to make out a word or phrase here and there: evidence, cash deposits, mal-something, could it be malpractice? Was Buzz suspicious of someone's malpractice? Was that someone in the firm, or was it someone in a company they did business with?

Keisha abruptly dropped the sheet of paper as if it were on fire. "Omigawd! Is this what got Buzz killed? He had something on somebody?"

She shoved the paper into her jeans' pocket, slammed the suitcase shut. She gave one last look around to be sure she hadn't missed anything.

She grabbed the bags, inched open the door, checked the hallway. It looked clear. She scooted out of the room, slammed the door behind her and hurried across the hall. While she was getting her key card out, Keisha thought she heard a noise. A door opening? Footsteps? She looked around wildly. The hall light was dim but all the doors she could see appeared to be tightly closed. She quickly slipped her card in place. The second it took for the green light to pop up seemed like minutes. She jerked her door open and shoved the bags inside. She quickly shut and locked her door, then leaned back against it with a sigh of relief.

When her breathing returned to normal, she still had to calm the turmoil in her mind. Her first thought was to run next door and show the paper to Fonnie. Her hand was on the door knob when she stopped, stepped back into the room and sank into a chair.

"But what if it's Paul or Amy that's involved in some illegal scheme?" The sound of her own voice in the empty room made her nervous. She wanted to talk to someone. But whom? She could call Stephon, ask him to come up. But something made her hesitate.

She began to wonder if what she'd found was really important after all. "It may be nothing. Just some silly scribbling like we all do from time to time. I guess I better sleep on it. Maybe it'll make more sense in the morning." She stood up. "Right now I've got to get Midge's card back to the desk clerk so they can clean up the room for new occupants."

Keisha didn't want to go back out, but knew she had to. She opened the door carefully, scanned up and down the hallway. She hurried to the elevator, pushed the button. She glanced at the floor indicator. The "L" was lit up. Probably being loaded with the new arrivals, she thought. She decided not to wait for it. Instead she dashed to the stairwell, flew down the steps, and gave Buzz's key to the desk clerk. He thanked her profusely, telling her about the many bus passengers that needed rooms. She listened politely and said that she was glad she could help.

When she got to the elevator, there was still a crowd of weary travelers lining up to get on. Keisha reluctantly turned back to the stairwell. She opened the door. She hesitated. The stairs were now dark. A bulb must have just burned out, she thought. She almost turned around to ask the clerk to replace it, but he was busy, and she didn't want to wait any longer. She took a deep breath, pulled up some reserve energy, and bounded up the stairs into the darkness. The door slammed shut behind her.

She was making the turn to the second floor when an arm across her chest stopped her sprint. And a hand across her mouth stifled her scream.

# SEVENTEEN

FONNIE WOKE UP Monday morning feeling a little more upbeat. At first she wondered why she felt better. Melanie was still missing. Buzz's death was still unexplained. The entire wedding party was under a cloud of uncertainty and possibly suspicion. But the sun was shining, the police were on the job, and she felt that progress was being made.

She reached for the phone. Last night Keisha said she'd stop by and get her on the way down to breakfast, but it was getting late and Fonnie was hungry. The phone rang several times before asking her to leave a message. "Keisha," Fonnie said, "I guess you're in the shower. I'm going to go ahead to the dining room. Come when you get ready."

As Fonnie headed for the dining room, she noticed the bus passengers who had checked in last evening were already on their way out. They seemed eager to assume their planned itinerary.

Jeremiah was finishing a stack of wheatcakes when Fonnie slid into the chair opposite him. He grinned at her. "Good morning, Sunshine. You're looking pert today."

"Now that's a word I haven't heard in years—an old-fashioned Southern word."

"If it was good enough for my grandpappy, it's good enough for me. I remember that's what he'd say to my grandma when she'd come in the kitchen with a lively step, humming snatches of songs."

"I can't say I'm in the humming mood, but I do feel livelier than I did yesterday. Maybe things aren't quite as bad as I imagined."

"I don't know about that. Clara's pretty upset."

"Oh, was she a good friend of Melanie?"

"It's not that. She's just worried about Tony. It seems he's been as jumpy as a grasshopper since the cops talked to him yesterday. Clara told me he left the search party early yesterday, made a run to the liquor store and was pretty smashed when she came in."

"She's upset about his drinking?"

"That, and the fact that apparently he was the last person to see Melanie Friday night. He insists he just escorted her to her room and that she was fine when he left her, but I'm not sure Clara is buying his story."

"Why wouldn't she?" Fonnie remembered Jeremiah had said earlier that the marriage was in trouble, but he hadn't gone into detail.

"It seems that Tony has had some indiscretions in the past," Jeremiah said. "I guess it's pretty hard for a woman to forget that."

The waitress came up and took Fonnie's order for oatmeal and cinnamon rolls. When they were alone again, Jeremiah went on. "Tony's a nice guy, a good provider, but I'm not sure he's cut out to be a family man. I think the coming baby has him worried. And I don't know what to think of his relationship with Melanie."

"Are you saying Tony may know more about Melanie's disappearance than he's letting on?"

"It's possible. At least I think Clara is nervous about it."

"Poor thing." Fonnie stirred another spoonful of sugar into her coffee. "I don't remember love being so complicated when I was young."

"And speaking of love complications," Jeremiah said, "here comes a young man who looks a little troubled."

Fonnie glanced up and watched Stephon as he hurried toward them. He did look troubled, Fonnie thought. Now what? Had he and Keisha had a spat already this morning?

Stephon pulled out a chair and slumped down like a collapsing balloon. He let out a long sigh and shook his head. "I don't understand women. I don't understand women at all."

Jeremiah nodded, "Join the club. Few men do understand the opposite sex. But what specifically is the problem now?"

"Either Keisha is hiding from me or just refusing to answer her phone and her door." Stephon wiped a hand across his chin and turned to Fonnie. "Have you talked to her this morning?"

Fonnie shook her head. "No. When I called and she didn't answer I figured she was in the shower. Of course, she could have come down early, and gone for a walk. What do you think, Jeremiah?"

Jeremiah scowled. He looked from Fonnie to Stephon and back again. "You mean, neither of you has seen or heard from Keisha since last night?"

They both shook their heads.

Jeremiah stood up and scooted his chair back so fast it started to tip over. He grabbed the chair and righted it. "I don't want to be an alarmist but I think we'd better check on her again. Doesn't she have a cell phone?"

Fonnie nodded. "Of course, if she'd gone out early for a beach walk she probably would've taken her cell."

Jeremiah dug his phone out of his pocket. "What's her number?"

Fonnie rattled it off, and prayed the phone would be answered.

After several rings, Jeremiah shook his head and snapped the phone shut. "Let's try her door again. If there's no answer, I think we'd better get the desk clerk to let us into her room." He paused. "No. On second thought, we'd better contact Lieutenant Steinberg, and let him check out the room."

Fonnie cupped her face in her hands and moaned. "Oh God," she cried, "do you think something may have happened to her."

"No, of course not." Jeremiah hesitated. "But with the things going on around here, we can't be too careful."

Stephon jumped up. His hands and his voice shook. "Let's go."

On their way out of the dining room, Fonnie noticed Hank, Doris, and Midge coming in. She gave them a slight nod and kept going.

When they reached Keisha's door, Stephon pounded repeatedly. The only response was an elderly gentleman down the hall sticking his head out to see what the racket was about.

Jeremiah motioned to Fonnie. "Go to your room and check your phone. Just in case she left a message."

Fonnie did as she was told and returned shortly with a shake of her head.

"Come on," Stephon said. "We're calling the police."

The trio waited in the lobby for them to arrive. The detective and two uniformed policemen drove up within ten minutes. Jeremiah explained about why they were worried. Fonnie was too distraught to say anything, and Stephon paced back and forth.

Lieutenant Steinberg listened without apparent emotion then signaled one of the cops with him to get the room key.

"Oh, dear. Oh, dear." The desk clerk shook his head in uncertainty. "I've got to call Mr. Myers about this. He'll be so upset."

"Yeah, sure," the young cop said. "Call your boss, but in the meantime give me the key."

The detective led the way to the elevator followed by Fonnie, Jeremiah, Stephon, and the uniformed policemen. No one said anything.

Fonnie kept her eyes on the floor, kept her hands clenched tightly, and tried to keep horrible thoughts out of her mind.

The group paused outside the door. Lieutenant Steinberg knocked loudly. The sound echoed down the hall, bounced off the low ceiling, pounded against Fonnie's ears. She held her breath, praying that Keisha's sleepy voice would answer the knock.

After a few seconds of silence, Steinberg motioned the others to stand back while he inserted the card key. Fonnie craned her neck to see inside the room as the door opened. She could only get a glimpse of the bed, but she could see the spread was pulled up. Either it hadn't been slept in, Fonnie thought, or it had been made up. Her thoughts tumbled over one another. It was too early for the motel maid to have made it up and she was sure Keisha wouldn't have bothered to do it.

Three pairs of eyes in the hallway followed the policemen as they surveyed the room, went into the bathroom, looked into the closet. Steinberg picked up a leather bag from the seat of a chair. He looked up at Fonnie in the doorway. "This her purse?"

Fonnie nodded.

The detective opened the bag, pulled out and examined a billfold. "Money, credit cards." He dug further and came out with a set of car keys. "Doesn't look like she drove anywhere."

Fonnie made no motion to go into the room. Although there didn't seem to be any sign of a struggle, she wondered if she was looking at a crime scene. Had Keisha disappeared as mysteriously and completely as Melanie?

She glanced at Stephon who stood close to her right elbow. If it were possible for a black man to look pale, he did. His face was contorted. He looked like a boxer who had just taken a blow to his gut. His shoulders slumped, his breathing came in ragged gasps. Fonnie reached over and touched his arm. She had had her doubts about Stephon the past few days, but now there was no doubt about the pain he was feeling.

Her attention turned back to the room when she heard the young cop say, "Lieutenant, check this out." The cop picked up something in a napkin. Fonnie could see that it looked like a piece of glass.

Steinberg left the closet he was examining and

crossed the room. "Hmm. Now why would she have saved half of a broken water glass?"

The young cop bent his head closer. "It's not a water glass, sir. It looks more like a highball glass. Maybe she was sharing drinks with someone in here."

The lieutenant looked toward the door. His gaze seemed to hover on Stephon. Steinberg turned back and barked out orders. "Bag it. Get the crew up here. Seal the room."

The detective went back over to the closet, bent down, examined the luggage and read the name tags. Fonnie promptly forgot about the glass when Steinberg walked over to her and asked, "Why does she have luggage labeled 'Cyrus Garrison'?"

"Cyrus? That must be Buzz. But I have no idea why she would have his luggage in her room. Maybe Midge, that's his wife, or rather his widow, would know."

"We'll see. In the meantime, I suggest you people stick around in the lobby until I have time to question everyone further."

Stephon leaned on the wall opposite Keisha's door. His head was tilted back and his eyes seemed fixed on the ceiling light fixture. Jeremiah went over to him. "Let's go downstairs. We can get a cup of coffee while we wait."

Stephon lowered his head and when he did, a tear rolled down his cheek. He nodded and trailed Jeremiah to the elevator.

When the elevator door opened, Edgar stormed off, and made a dash toward the policeman. "What in the hell has happened now?"

# EIGHTEEN

KEISHA WAS COLD. Her body trembled like a leaf in a frigid windstorm. She wrapped her arms around herself, felt the goose flesh, the icy skin. She needed a blanket. There should be a blanket someplace here in her room if only she could find it. It was so dark. What had happened to the night light in the bathroom? And what had happened to her bed? It was so hard. She moved her right hand to feel under her hips. The bed felt like a cement sidewalk, hard and cold and unyielding. She tried to turn to see if any light was creeping in through the window drapes. A sharp pain jerked her head back. She let out a low whimper and the sound scraped her throat. She tried to swallow but the effort brought tears to her eyes. Her throat was parched. She touched the front of her neck and winced in pain.

Her thoughts whirled around as in a miasma. Where was she? This wasn't her bed, her room. Why was it so dark? What had happened? Why did her throat feel like it was in vise? If only she could have a drink of water. If only she could cry out for help. She opened her mouth but the only sound that came out was a low raspy groan. She needed to remember what had happened. But her mind rebelled. The effort was too great. She sank back into a swamp of unconsciousness.

FONNIE LED STEPHON out to the motel verandah and motioned to some chairs. He shook his head. "I can't sit. I've got to walk. I've got to think. I've got to do something."

He took off toward the pier, his face lifted up to the sky, his hands raised as if in supplication. Fonnie followed at a distance. She knew she couldn't keep up with him, but neither did she want him out of her sight. She didn't know why. His grief and despair seemed genuine, but did he know something he hadn't mentioned, or did he have suspicions about someone?

They reached the pier. Fonnie slumped on the nearest bench to catch her breath while Stephon stalked out to the end. The sky had become overcast and a cold breeze blew in from the ocean. Even though she had a sweater on, Fonnie shivered. She looked up and down the beach and wondered if the police would duplicate the search they had done the day before. There had been no sign of the missing Melanie. If the same person was responsible for the disappearance of both girls, it seemed likely they were being held in the same place. Fonnie closed her eyes and shook her head to drive out the horrible thought that both their bodies would be found in the same place.

When she opened her eyes, they came to rest on the statue of the Shepherd by the Sea. The front of the chapel faced the beach and the Shepherd was holding forth his hands in blessing to those who sailed there. The beach side of the chapel seemed much closer to the motel than the street side. Fonnie couldn't see the Shepherd's face clearly, but she remembered His smile and felt His compassion.

She began to sob. Tears had never come easily to her. A lifetime of self-restraint and a nursing career that commanded emotional control, seldom allowed her the relief of crying. Now she gave way completely. What had started as a professional relationship between Fonnie and Keisha had transformed into a deep friendship. Keisha had nagged and bullied Fonnie into learning to walk again after her stroke, had pushed her into independence. And even though there were times Fonnie lashed out at the young girl, she knew Keisha was doing it out of love.

Now Keisha was gone and Fonnie could do nothing except cry and pray to the Shepherd by the Sea.

Staring at the chapel, Fonnie was suddenly reminded of Keisha's father. He was a preacher, the minister of a large African-American church in Groverton. He had to be notified of Keisha's disappearance, as did her brother, Tyrone. Tyrone Riggs, even though he was still in high school, had also become a close friend of Fonnie's. He did her yard work and general maintenance around the house. They had often laughed together over his passion for big words. Tyrone would never describe a person as being "nice." The person would be "amiable" or "winsome" or "congenial" but never just plain "nice."

She got up from the bench, found a tissue in her pocket, wiped her eyes and her nose. Crying time was over. She had to make some telephone calls. She took a deep breath and started back to the motel, then glanced to the end of the pier. Stephon was leaning against the railing, his head bent down. She had no doubt that he also was praying.

Fonnie didn't see Lieutenant Steinberg when she entered the lobby, but a uniformed officer was standing by the front desk. She went up and told him she was going to her room and they could reach her there if they had any new information. The officer gave her a polite nod but not an encouraging one. She sensed there would be no information any time soon.

Fonnie decided to call Brian first. Since he was going to be working the evening shift this week, he'd be home now.

Fonnie's hands trembled as she punched in her home phone number. Brian answered on the second ring. His slow "Hello" sounded as if he expected further bad news.

"Oh Brian." Fonnie's voice cracked before she could say anything else.

"What?" Brian nearly shouted. "Have they found Melanie? What's going on?"

Fonnie sucked up a gob of air, tried to control her emotions. "It's so terrible."

"What's terrible. Tell me!"

"Now Keisha's missing. She's gone. Just like Melanie. Not a trace." Fonnie couldn't keep back the sobs that tore at her.

"Gram, pull yourself together. Tell me exactly what happened."

Fonnie did her best to explain. She told him of Keisha's empty room, of the bed not being slept in, of there being no sign of a struggle. "It's like she just walked out into thin air and disappeared."

"I'm coming up. You need to have someone with you. I'll call in to work and explain it's a family emergency."

"Yes. I need you here. But first you have to call Reverend Riggs. I don't know what you're going to tell him. Since his wife died, he seems to have depended on Keisha. This is going to be so hard for him—and for Tyrone. Poor Tyrone."

"I'll go over and see them. Since this is a school holiday, Tyrone will probably be home. I'll tell them about Keisha and then I'm coming up. I'll be there this afternoon—as soon as I can. In the meantime, try to stay calm. The police will find her—they'll find both of them." Brian tried to put a smile in his voice. "Like you used to tell me, 'Keep the faith.'"

"I'm trying."

As Fonnie hung up the phone, she heard a soft knock on the door. A tremor of fear shot through her body. Was it a policeman, she thought, with news—bad news? She stood up slowly, made her way to the door, and squinted into the peephole. She gave a sigh of relief and quickly opened the door to Jeremiah.

"Didn't mean to run out on you," she said, "but I had to make a telephone call."

"Brian?"

"Yes. He's going to notify Keisha's family and then come up here."

"Good. Now let me fill you in on what I've learned about last night."

Fonnie stepped back into the room, sat down on the side of the bed, and motioned Jeremiah to a chair. Her voice cracked. "What did you find out?"

He explained to her about Midge's request, about Keisha packing up Buzz's clothes, and then taking the key card to the desk clerk.

"Did the clerk see where she went after handing in the key?"

"No. He was too busy checking in the bus passengers."

"But somebody must have seen her," Fonnie said. "Seen what direction she went in. If she was with anybody. What are the police doing?"

"I guess they're doing whatever they're supposed to do—interviewing people, asking questions. I know they took Buzz's bags that Keisha packed. So they're probably going through them. And I overheard Steinberg give instructions to contact the Wilmington police to question those on the bus in case they saw anything. Melanie's picture is already on the TV news and Keisha's will be shortly. I guess all we can do now is wait—and pray."

"I suppose Detective Steinberg has checked all our friends for alibis."

"I suppose."

"And," Fonnie said, "do you think he'll share that information with me?"

"That's a definite 'no'."

"So I guess we'll have to start our own list." Fonnie reached for the pad of motel stationery and a pen. "Now you told me that Clara said Tony was smashed last evening when she went to their room. I take that to mean he was drunk."

"I think that's the definition. But don't ask me if he was dead drunk or passed out or just tipsy because I don't know."

"We can find out. What I really want to know is whether Clara saw him before or after the time Keisha disappeared."

"Probably before. I saw her come up to the verandah with a bunch of other searchers. I remember thinking she looked pretty bushed and that she shouldn't have been out there all day—being in the family way like she is. I'm not sure if she got anything to eat or not. She may have gone right up to their room. If so, that would have been when Keisha was eating with you. I can ask Clara to be sure."

"And there's one other thing you need to ask."

"What's that?"

"Did Tony go out again?"

Jeremiah grimaced. "Okay, now we have Tony on the hot seat, what about Stephon? Where did he go after he said goodnight? Straight to bed like a good little boy? Or did he follow Keisha? Maybe arranged to meet her later? Did they meet and have a lover's spat that turned violent?"

With each of Jeremiah's questions, Fonnie's head dropped lower. When her friend paused, she looked up. "I don't know. But I do think his grief is genuine. You saw how he looked. Could he be that good an actor if he wasn't really hurting?"

Jeremiah walked to the window, gazed out for a long moment before answering. "Yes, he's hurting. But is it because of Keisha's disappearance, or because of what he did to make her disappear?"

Fonnie dropped the pen and paper in her lap. "None of it makes any sense. Is it all connected? Or do we have three separate mysteries? Buzz's death, Melanie's disappearance, and now Keisha?"

# NINETEEN

KEISHA HAD TO PEE. Somehow this basic animal urge worked itself through her unconsciousness. She raised her head, pushed herself to a sitting position, and tried to swing her legs over the side of the bed. But there was no side of the bed. Her legs scraped across cold concrete. She opened her eyes and saw only darkness. Her fuzzy brain tried to make sense of the situation. It couldn't. Her head ached, her throat felt raw, and she had no idea where she was. She leaned back on her elbows, and when she tilted her face upward, she glimpsed a tiny strip of light.

She forced herself to focus on the light. It was coming from somewhere. Another room? Outside? Wherever the origin of the light, she reasoned the space beneath it had to be a wall. If she could get to her feet and walk toward the light, she would come to the wall. Then she could follow the wall around to a light switch or a door. She had to get out of this place soon and find a bathroom or she was going to wet her pants.

The first step was to get up. She bent her knees and at the same time pushed her body back into a sitting position. She then leaned to the right, gave a mighty push with her right hand and came up on both knees. Her head began to spin, and she was afraid of toppling over, but she took some deep breaths and regained her balance. So far, so good.

Next she had to figure out how to get from her knees to her feet. It should be a simple task, she thought, but then her mind started playing games with her. One part of her brain told her to forget it, to lie back down, to go back to sleep. It seemed like a marvelous idea.

But then another voice was telling her not to give up. It sounded like her father's voice. "All things are possible," he said.

Keisha smiled in the darkness, and her spirit answered him. "Sure, Pop, I can do it. I know I can do it." She raised her left knee and placed her left foot flat on the floor. Then she put both hands on her left knee and pushed up with her other leg. She was standing. She wanted to shout "Hallelujah" but when she opened her mouth no sound came out. She wondered why she couldn't talk, but there wasn't time to think about that now. She had to get to the wall.

After a few moments her head stopped reeling, and she took a step forward. Then another and another. She was going to make it. She pushed her hands out in front of her so they would touch the wall first. At the same time her hands reached the rough cement wall, her shins collided with something hard. She bent down, rubbed the front of her legs, and then felt forward to find what she'd run into. It was a bench, a wooden bench. Steadying herself with one hand against the wall, she turned around and sank gratefully onto the seat.

She tried to twist her head to the light. Every movement of her neck was agony, but she had to see where the light was coming from. Then she attempted to hold her head still and twist her whole upper body until she got a good view. It seemed to be a slight crack between the top of the wall and the ceiling of the room. It has to be sunlight, she thought. This is an outside wall and there must be people out there—people who could help. She listened carefully for voices, for any sound. There was nothing. She dropped her head down in despair.

Again her mind tried to escape from the prison that held her body, but something deep within Keisha's soul resisted. Somehow she would find a way out.

She leaned back against the wall hoping her head would stop swimming. After a while it slowed enough so that she thought it safe to move again. Instead of standing up, she slid gingerly down the bench, one hand leading the way so she wouldn't tumble over the end. The other hand brushed over the cement wall. She would stay with the bench as long as it lasted and one way or another she would cover every inch of the wall. There had to be a light switch somewhere and there had to be a door—a door to freedom. It took only a few seconds to reach the first corner. The bench continued and so did Keisha. After moving a few feet along the second wall, her fingers dropped off the end of the wooden seat.

She slowly heaved herself up and started walking, her hands continually brushing the wall. Before long she felt a change in texture under her fingers. She puzzled over it. She rubbed over the surface again. Were her hands becoming as numb as her brain? In a moment both her hands and her mind kicked into gear.

She was feeling a smoother, warmer surface. She had found a door.

Frantically, she groped in front of her. Where there was a door, there had to be a knob. Her left wrist found it with a bang. She shook her wrist in pain while her right hand grasped the metal knob. She took a deep breath and turned the knob. She heard a slight squeak. She held the knob tightly and pulled it hard toward her. The door didn't move.

Keisha had to fight the despair that again threatened to engulf her. She yanked on the doorknob, over and over. Nothing. Her head was beginning to feel like a whirling top. She leaned forward to rest. She felt a movement. The door was opening, but instead of moving toward her, as she had expected, it was moving away from her body. Keisha bent forward and moved with it. She jerked herself up. Maybe this was her way out. She wanted to smile. She wanted to laugh. Both were impossible. Every motion of her face and neck brought spasms of pain. But that wasn't going to stop her now.

She pushed hard against the door. It slammed open with a resounding noise. It had apparently hit another wall. She kept her left hand on the door and stepped into what she thought was an open space. Again her legs bumped into a solid object. Another bench? She felt around and this time her hands felt something smooth and round. Her brain sent a welcomed message to her bladder. She had found a bathroom.

She turned around, pulled down her jeans. When she finished, her fingers searched for the flushing mechanism, but couldn't find one. That's all right, she thought. At least now she could focus on what was really important—how to get out. Perhaps she'd even be able to remember how she got here.

She stood up quickly. Too quickly. The inside of her head spun around violently. She wobbled as she zipped up her jeans and reached out to the door. Her goal was to get back to further search along the wall. She didn't make it.

She staggered sideways, fell, and her head smashed against the concrete floor.

# TWENTY

IT WAS NEARLY two o'clock that Monday afternoon when Brian drove up to the Beachside Motel. Fonnie and Jeremiah had dragged their rocking chairs to the far side of the verandah that had a view of the parking lot so they could keep watch. As soon as she saw him drive in, Fonnie rushed for the lobby. Jeremiah was right behind her.

Brian burst through the front doors and headed for the desk. His grandmother's voice whirled him around. "Brian. Over here."

He closed the distance between them in a nanosecond and enfolded her in his long arms. He stepped back and asked, "Any news?"

She shook her head, then looking past his shoulder, she spied another figure entering the door. Fonnie pulled out of Brian's arms into another outstretched pair. "Tyrone. I'm so glad you came."

The big brown hunk squeezed her and said between tight lips, "I had to. I have to find Sis."

"I know," Fonnie said. Ever since she'd met him, Fonnie had been impressed with Tyrone's caring attitude and tenderness. At sixteen, he had the body of a bear, the mind of a scholar, and the heart of a Santa Claus.

She pulled him over to Jeremiah and introduced

them. "This is Keisha's little brother, Tyrone." Fonnie turned back to the young man. "And this is Jeremiah Trent, my new son-in-law's uncle who has become a good friend."

"Little doesn't seem to be the right adjective for you, young man," Jeremiah said as the two shook hands. "But I'm mighty glad to meet you. I only wish we had some good news."

Brian reached out and grasped Jeremiah's hand. "Thanks for being here for Gram. I know it's been a comfort to her."

Jeremiah nodded. "It's been bad, Brian. Two young women missing and not a clue. Or if there is, the police are being close-mouthed about it."

Brain looked over at two uniformed officers by the desk. "I'm going to see if I can get up with Steinberg and get the latest."

"I'm going with you," Tyrone said with a determined look.

Brian hesitated. "Better let me go first. Since I'm in law enforcement, the detective is more apt to be open with me. He sounded like an okay guy when I talked to him on the phone."

Tyrone shook his head. "She's my sister. I have a right to know what's going on."

"And you will. But let me handle it. Cops have to be careful when they talk to family. They may clam up around you." Brian turned to Fonnie. "You and Jeremiah show Tyrone around, fill him in on all you know. And get rooms for us. I'll catch up with you later."

"Before you leave," Fonnie said to Brian, "there's something you need to know. The detective has been doing quick interviews with people all morning. But he spent an awful long time with Stephon. And when Stephon came out he wouldn't talk to me. Said he was going to his room. Maybe you could find out about that."

Brain frowned, shook his head and forged over to the police officers.

"Who's this Stephon?" Tyrone asked.

Fonnie and Jeremiah exchanged glances. Fonnie started to say something, but Jeremiah answered first. "A friend of your sister's." He took Tyrone by the elbow and steered him toward the verandah. "Let's get some fresh air and I'll tell you about everybody."

The sun had come out and the air was pleasantly warm. A gentle breeze was blowing in from the ocean. Fonnie thought how outwardly serene everything seemed, in sharp contrast to her inner turmoil.

They were barely settled in their chairs when Tyrone demanded, "Now tell me about this Stephon fellow and anyone else who might be a suspect. Brian told me what he knew on the way up, but I want to hear it from you."

"Take it easy," Jeremiah said. "As far as we know, no one is a suspect yet, unless Brian can get some information out of the cops. But I will tell you what has happened that we know. I think we need to start with Melanie's disappearance and go from there."

"No," Fonnie interrupted, "you need to go back to the wedding and Buzz's death. I'm sure somehow it's all connected."

For the next several minutes Jeremiah related the events of the past several days with occasional interjections from Fonnie. Tyrone listened with his whole body.

When they were finished, Tyrone sat hunched over, his fingers clenched together, his eyes misty. "Why would anyone want to hurt Keisha?"

Fonnie had no answer. She wanted to say that maybe Keisha hadn't been hurt, that she would turn up soon, that everything would be fine. But she didn't believe it and she knew Tyrone wouldn't either. She evaded the question with a quick change of subject. "I meant to ask about your father sooner. How is he?"

Tyrone turned to her and gave a faint smile. "Living his faith. He's called a prayer meeting of the entire church. He wanted to come with us, but decided he would be more help to Keisha by manning the prayer fortress. Said he would keep people praying until Keisha was found and returned to her family."

"And she will be," Jeremiah said. "Prayer is a powerful force. And in the meantime, we'll be doing a little sleuthing ourselves. I think there's one area the police may have failed to consider."

Fonnie jerked up. "What are you talking about, Jeremiah? You know something I don't?"

"Not really, but it occurred to me that officially Buzz's death isn't even a police case yet. Therefore, they may not be considering any connection between him and the disappearances. We, however, think there is a connection. So maybe if we learn more about Buzz, we'll spot a link."

"But you've known Buzz ever since Paul joined the law firm," Fonnie said.

"Only socially. I don't know anything about his law practice, and at this point, I don't want to call Paul and ask him any questions."

"So how are you going to learn anything?"

Jeremiah clapped Tyrone on the back. "That's where this young man comes in."

"Me?" Tyrone sounded surprised. "What can I do?"

"If you're like most kids today, you're computer savvy. Right?"

"Sure. What did you have in mind?"

"The motel has computers with Internet connections for patrons to use. You're going to do a search for the law firm of Myers, Garrison, and Trent with special attention to Cyrus Garrison. Find out where he went to school, his particular branch of law, anything else that might give us a clue. Are you up to it?"

"Yes sir, if it will facilitate the investigation." Tyrone grinned shyly. "I saw a coffee shop as I came in. Let me appropriate a Milky Way first. I google faster with an elevated glucose level."

When Tyrone was out of earshot, Jeremiah shook his head at Fonnie. "Does he always use five-dollar words? He sounds like a walking dictionary."

"I know. He's studying for his SAT, and he thinks he needs to improve his vocabulary."

"I may have to improve mine," Jeremiah said, "if I stick around him long."

Fonnie grinned. "It wouldn't hurt you any. But back to the matter at hand, do you think you'll find any useful information on the Internet?"

"Never can tell. At least it'll make Tyrone feel that he's helping."

Fonnie watched her young friend and her older friend walk toward the computer lounge, their heads together as they discussed their project. In a way she envied them. At least they were doing something, while she sat there on her tush. She waited impatiently for Brian to come back and report to her. Or maybe he won't be back any time soon, she thought. He would probably stick close to Lieutenant Steinberg as long as he was allowed to.

She was squirming in her chair wondering what to do next when she spotted Lula on the far end of the verandah. The young woman was sipping from a tall frosty glass and Fonnie was sure it wasn't lemonade. She liked Lula but worried about her drinking. Fonnie suspected that Lula and Edgar's marriage had problems, and this might be Lula's way of coping.

Lula looked in Fonnie's direction, waved, and motioned her over. Fonnie waved back and started toward her. It would be better to have someone to talk to, she thought, rather than sitting in a funk all by herself.

"You been left alone like I have?" Fonnie asked as she pulled up a chair.

"It's just as well. Edgar's not been fit company since Melanie's gone missing." Lula sipped her drink and then quickly added, "And, of course, Keisha's disappearance has upset him greatly too. As it has me. I'm so sorry. Keisha was a nice kid."

Fonnie felt that Lula was being genuinely sympathetic. She appreciated it, but bristled at the past tense. "Keisha *is* a nice kid," she said, "not *was*."

Lula's hand flew to her mouth. "I'm sorry. I didn't mean that. I'm sure she'll be found soon."

Fonnie leaned back in her chair. "And I'm sorry I snapped at you. It's a bad time for all of us." Her thoughts went to Tyrone. It had to be an especially hard time for him. She was glad Jeremiah had taken an interest in him.

Lula's voice brought Fonnie's mind back from it's wanderings. "As I was telling Stephon," Lula said, "the two cases are different."

Fonnie jerked to attention. "When were you talking to Stephon? And why are the cases different?"

"Stephon was wandering around like a lost puppy when the police got through with him. I offered him a drink and a listening ear. He refused the drink but spent ten minutes telling me how much he loved Keisha." Lula paused. "Oops. I mean how much he *loves* Keisha—present tense."

"You think he's sincere?"

"Yes, I do. I'm pretty good at reading men." Lula gave Fonnie a rueful smile. "Which," she went on, "can be a mixed blessing."

Fonnie let the enigmatic comment pass. "So what makes the two disappearances different?"

"Whatever happened to Melanie was of her own doing. I don't mean she deliberately took a powder, but it was the result of an illicit rendezvous or something crooked. Unlike Keisha, she is *not* a nice person."

"And," Fonnie said, "you think Keisha was just in the wrong place at the wrong time?"

Lula nodded. "Something like that."

"I take it you didn't like Melanie."

Lula drained her glass before answering. "She was a scheming, greedy, money-grabbing man-eater." She gave a loud laugh. "And that was her good side."

Fonnie could tell Lula was definitely tipsy. Was her description of Melanie valid? Or was the alcohol exaggerating a case of marital jealousy? Maybe she should fan the flames a little more, Fonnie thought, and see what else came out. She put on her a naive expression. "But I had the idea that Edgar and Melanie were good friends."

"Hell, yes, they were good friends. Every time she'd come to Richmond the two of them were like cozy cousins."

"She came to Richmond often?"

"Every few months. Supposedly to visit her dear Uncle Hank and go over her investments with Tony. But she always seemed to have some legal problem she had to discuss with Edgar—as if they didn't have lawyers in Miami. During her Christmas visit here, Edgar and Melanie huddled together like they were planning a big business deal. I finally told her to shove off and leave my husband alone." Lula swirled a single ice cube around in her glass. Fonnie could feel the pain in her voice as she said, "Edgar was furious with me."

Lula jumped up and slung the ice cube over the railing. "I need a refill, and since Edgar doesn't have his liquor license yet, I have to get it from my private supply. So if you'll excuse me…." She stood and bent her head close to Fonnie. "Wanna know a secret?" she whispered.

"Sure," Fonnie said. "I'm always open to secrets."

"I heard Melanie telling people she came to the wedding because she wanted to spend more time with Stephon. I know for a fact that's a lie. She and Edgar had already planned a tryst." With that pronouncement, Lula stumbled her way inside the motel.

Fonnie became lost in thought. Keisha's disappearance had nearly preempted her concern for Melanie. Now the faces of both women stared at her through the cumulus clouds. One black, one white, one sweet, one not-so-sweet, both pleading for help. And there's not a thing I can do.

The sound of footsteps brought her mind back. She turned and leaned forward eagerly as Brian came up to her. "Learn anything?" she asked.

He shook his head. "Not really. They've sent the broken highball glass found in Keisha's room to the crime lab." He flopped down in a chair and frowned at her. "You didn't mention the glass to me, Gram. Didn't you know about it?"

"I do remember them looking at a piece of glass, but Steinberg didn't mention it to me. Is it important?"

"It might be. Fingerprints. And Steinberg said there seemed to be the residue of some substance in it."

"Substance? What does substance mean in cop talk?"

"Maybe a drug."

"Keisha would never take drugs. You know her, Brian. You tell that detective Keisha is as clean as new snow."

"I did. But she may have had a visitor who wasn't all that clean."

Fonnie took a ragged breath. "It's all so terrible. Do the police think the same person is responsible for both disappearances?"

"Steinberg didn't say so, but I think they're working under that assumption." Brian glanced around the verandah. "What happened to Tyrone? I wanted him to go with me when I interviewed Stephon."

"He's in the computer lounge. Jeremiah put him to work." Fonnie went on to explain what they planned to do. She squinted at him. "Why are you interviewing Stephon? And why do you want Tyrone with you?"

"Stephon seems like a good place to start. He may know something he hasn't told or doesn't realize is significant. And he may talk more freely with Keisha's brother there."

"True. But until Tyrone gets back, you could start with Tony Cauthen. His name keeps cropping up in connection with Melanie. It may be nothing, but you need to explore it." Fonnie gazed out to the calm ocean and tried to steal some of its serenity. It helped a little. She then turned back to Brian. "But don't talk to him in front of Clara. She's pregnant and I don't want anything upsetting her."

"You think Tony's account of his actions would upset her?"

"It's possible," Fonnie said.

# TWENTY-ONE

THE POUNDING INSIDE Keisha's head was incessant. She pushed herself to a sitting position and cradled her head in her hands. She felt something warm and sticky and realized it was blood, but it didn't seem to matter to her. She knew she'd fallen and had probably blacked out again. She wondered how long she'd been unconscious. She lifted her head, and as she did so, the pain in her neck and throat eclipsed any other thought. If only she could get a drink of water.

She remembered she was in a bathroom. A bathroom meant a sink, running water. She reached behind her, grasped the edge of the commode, and pulled herself up. Her hands groped in the darkness until they came in contact with something solid—something that dipped in the center. She fumbled for the faucets, found them, tried to turn them. They didn't move. Maybe her hands were too slippery. She wiped both hands across her shirt, grabbed the faucets again. She leaned against the sink to balance herself and willed every bit of her energy to open the water spigots. She felt a slight movement under her right hand. She kept up the turning motion and in a few moments she heard the trickle of water.

Keisha paused just long enough to breathe a prayer

of thanks before immersing her hands in the blessed flow. She cupped both hands under the spigot, felt them fill up. Trembling, she brought her hands to her lips. The water caressed her chapped lips and dribbled down the front of her shirt. With the next hand full, she opened her lips and poured water into her mouth. At first the coolness felt wonderful, but when she tried to swallow, the pain was overwhelming. She clenched at her throat, gagged, and spit out most of the water.

At that moment, as her own hands touched her neck, she remembered what had happened in the darkened stairwell.

She had been bounding up the steps to return to her room when she was grabbed from behind. An arm tightened across her chest. A hand covered her mouth. She started kicking and thrashing. Her resistance was short lived as powerful hands girdled her neck, squeezing tighter and tighter.

Now, as the horrific memory flooded over her, Keisha dropped her hands to her sides, leaned against the sink. She took short, quick breaths, tried to control her emotions. She slowly lifted one hand and followed the slight indentation on the side of her neck. Someone had tried to choke her death. Maybe he thought he'd succeeded. Or maybe, after she'd lost consciousness he'd tossed her into this room, and simply left her to die.

Those hands. There had been something familiar about those hands. She couldn't remember what it was, but she knew those hands had touched her at a previous time.

Before she could follow that train of thought, another memory popped to the forefront of her brain.

She recalled why she had been in the stairwell. She'd taken Buzz's room key to the desk clerk after clearing out the room. Keisha remembered neatly packing Buzz's clothes, and placing his suitcases in the back of her closet. And she remembered one more thing—the piece of paper. The paper covered with Buzz's comments and question marks. The paper she'd crammed into her jeans' pocket. The paper she'd planned to think about later.

She slowly lowered both hands and explored all her pockets. They were empty. The paper was gone.

FONNIE LOOKED UP in surprise as Tyrone lumbered out of the lobby, came up to her and Brian. She inched forward in her chair. "Where did you lose Jeremiah?"

"Not to worry. I finished my reconnaissance mission. Didn't find anything advantageous to us, but Jeremiah wanted to look some more. I gave him the search engine speed course. I think he's become enamored with the Internet. He said he'd be here shortly, but I wouldn't count on it." Tyrone slumped in a rocker. He turned to Brian. "Anything new to report?"

"No, but you and I are going to do a little investigating of our own. There's a couple of guys I want to chat with."

Fonnie waved them off. "Good luck. I'll wait here for Jeremiah."

Several minutes later she saw Jeremiah coming her way. He was rubbing his eyes. "How was your trek into cyberspace?" Fonnie asked.

"Fascinating. It's amazing what one can learn about another person."

"So what *did* you learn about Buzz?"

"He specializes in personal injury cases and he's a member of the Million Dollar Forum."

"Million Dollar Forum? What on earth is that?"

"It's a group of trial lawyers who have received a verdict or settlement for their clients of one million dollars or more."

"Wow," Fonnie said, "I had Buzz pegged for a buffoon. He must have been more impressive in a courtroom than in social situations."

"Apparently, but I don't think we've come any closer to finding a motive for murder. I guess it was a crazy idea."

"Not at all. We have to follow our instincts, no matter how harebrained they may seem."

Jeremiah's eyebrows shot up. "You sound as if you may have a harebrained scheme lurking in that lovely head of yours."

"I may," Fonnie said.

"So out with it."

"What we need to think about is the 'why' of Keisha's abduction." When Jeremiah made no comment, Fonnie went on. "Lula said that Keisha was in the wrong place at the wrong time. Which, to my mind, means she accidentally came across some incriminating evidence against somebody. That somebody found out and took measures to get rid of the evidence and maybe of Keisha."

Jeremiah nodded his head. "I agree. So we work backwards to where Keisha could have come up with this evidence."

"Right. And the only logical place would have been in Buzz's room when she packed his bags."

"But the police have those bags now," Jeremiah said, "and if they found anything there, they're not letting it be known."

"Of course they didn't find anything. Keisha kept it on her person. So we figure out who knew Keisha was going to Buzz's room, or who may have seen her go in there."

"Fonnie, I'm sure the police have figured that out and have questioned every possible suspect. What more can we do?"

"Not we—you," Fonnie said. "You are going to talk to those same suspects. Only instead of trying to get information, you are going to give it."

"But I don't have any information."

"Yes, you do. You know that Keisha came to my room before she went downstairs with Buzz's key."

"But she didn't." Jeremiah stared hard at Fonnie. "Did she?"

"No, she didn't. But you could start that rumor and give the guilty party something to worry about. He may wonder if Keisha told me something or gave me something to hold for her. He might get so worried, he'd try to search my room and we could set a trap for him."

"Whoa there. Speaking of crazy ideas, that one tops the list. You'd be setting yourself up as a target. Brian would have my head if I went along with that."

Fonnie gave a loud sigh. "I guess you're right. Forget I said anything." At the same time Fonnie was apparently submitting to Jeremiah's common sense, she was planning how to spread the rumor herself. She had to do something to shake things up and perhaps make the villain show himself—or herself.

As daylight dwindled, the breeze became cooler. Fonnie gave a slight shiver. "I need to go inside. Want to find a cup of coffee?"

"Not now. I'll catch up with you later. I'm going to wander down the street, check out the stores, find out what the scuttlebutt is. Something new may surface."

Fonnie slowly made her way inside, pondering her next move. She realized the tale she planned to tell needed an adjustment. If the bad guy had seen Keisha exit Buzz's room, then he knew she'd not come to Fonnie's room. But it was possible that when Keisha took Buzz's suitcases to her room, she could have phoned Fonnie. That's it, Fonnie thought. She'd tell people she had received a phone call from Keisha—that she couldn't remember exactly what Keisha had said because she'd been half asleep. But maybe she'd remember later, and when she did, she would tell the police. Fonnie nodded her head in satisfaction. That ought to be enough to put the perp on edge, she thought.

As luck would have it, she had a chance to put her plan into action immediately. Hank, Doris, and Midge were just entering the front door. Fonnie sat down on one of the sofas and beckoned them over. They approached her as if she were the chief mourner at a wake. Doris eased down next to her and grasped her hand. "We're so sorry about Keisha. After the police talked to us, we felt as if we simply had to get out for a while. We took a long drive up the coast."

Hank pulled up a chair, brushed a hand over his thinning hair. "We thought about asking you to come along, but figured you'd want to stay on the spot—in case anything new came up, you know."

"Of course," Fonnie said. "But thank you for thinking of me. Actually, there may be something new if only I could get my poor memory to kick in."

"What do you mean," Midge asked.

That was Fonnie's opening to proceed with her scheme to flush out the villain. None of the three people in front of her were suspects in her mind, but she knew this conversation would make the rounds until the intended person heard it. She had no idea what would happen after that. But she was positive, whatever happened, she would be ready for it.

# TWENTY-TWO

KEISHA GROPED HER WAY out of the bathroom and found another bench on the other side of the door. She desperately wanted a drink of water, but wasn't able to bear the pain of trying to swallow it.

She knew a little anatomy and wondered how her attacker had injured her throat so badly without crushing her windpipe. How come she couldn't swallow and couldn't talk but she was still able to breathe? Maybe the short while she'd been able to struggle dislodged his hands enough to save her life. In any case, she wasn't going to give up now. She had to find her way out of this prison.

She twisted her body to see if the fragment of light was still there. It was, but it was dimmer. The day was fading. It would soon be night again. Would that make it twenty-four hours she'd been in this dungeon? Probably, however there was no time to think of that now. If there was a way in here, there had to be a way out.

She started scooting along the bench again, this time along the opposite wall, searching for another door or a light switch. The bench came to an end where the wall turned the other corner. Keisha stood up and kept going, feeling her way along the wall. She had gone only a short distance when her foot bumped into an object. It was a soft object—perhaps a bag of some kind. She bent down to shove it out of her way.

Her fingers felt a piece of fabric. She followed the smoothness until her hand met something cold and round—an arm. She gasped. Her hand flew up. She toppled to the floor and dropped her head on her knees. A moan escaped through her lips. She recoiled at the thought of what she had touched. Someone else had also been thrown into this hellhole—left to die as she had been. But was the person dead? She had to find out.

It was several minutes before Keisha forced herself to touch the arm again. Her fingers found the fabric and moved upward. She felt a face, probably a feminine face, and long strands of hair. She held her hand over the face, could feel no breaths from the mouth. She felt for a carotid pulse as she'd been taught in her CPR class. Nothing. She was sharing her cell with a dead girl.

Her hand moved back down the arm, came to the wrist, collided with something metallic and she heard a faint tinkle. Her fingers explored a bracelet and she could make out a fish and a lion. It had to be Melanie's zodiac charm bracelet.

She swayed back and forth as she held tightly to Melanie's hand. It was soft and spongy. Since Melanie had been missing a full day before Keisha had been attacked herself, she realized that rigor mortis must have already come and gone. She faintly remembered learning that rigor mortis was only a temporary rigidity of the muscles after death and that after several hours the muscles again relaxed.

Her other hand found the silver ring that held lip gloss. Keisha had been amused when she first saw the charm bracelet and the ring. Imagine glamorous, sophisticated Melanie wearing jewelry meant for a teenager. She wished now she'd told Melanie that it was a beautiful bracelet—wished she'd told her that she was a beautiful person. But it was too late.

Keisha's fingers fondled the ring; her mind pictured the lip gloss inside. She bit her own parched, chapped lips and imagined how wonderful it would be to apply a bit of the emollient. She didn't think Melanie would mind sharing. She found the clasp, pushed it. The ring snapped open. Keisha twirled a finger around inside expecting to find a soothing salve. Instead she touched only hard metal. There was no salve, no lubricant for her arid lips. She dug all around inside the ring. Maybe she could find a tiny trace left in a corner. All she found was what felt like a fine powder. She didn't know what to make of it. She withdrew her finger, wiped it on her trouser leg, and snapped the lid shut.

One of her father's favorite hymns floated through her head, *There is a Balm in Gilead.* But there was no balm for her today. The disappointment was too much to bear.

Tears slid down her cheeks. Somehow, they brought a measure of relief. It felt good to cry—to cry for Melanie, to cry for herself, to cry for lost futures.

WHEN FONNIE FINISHED telling her story of Keisha's phone call the night before and that she couldn't recall what Keisha had said, Midge dismissed her concern with a wave of her hand. "It couldn't have been important. Don't worry about it."

Hank nodded in agreement. "You just need to relax

and take it easy. Things have been pretty rough for you today."

Fonnie smiled at the trio. "You're right. Maybe I need to give my brain a rest. I'm going to my room and take a nap."

"Good idea," Doris said.

Fonnie had no intention of actually taking a nap, but when she got to her room, she felt every bit of energy slip away. Maybe she had better rest, she thought. She would need to be at her

best for whatever came next.

She took off her shoes, stretched out on the bed.

The shrilling of the phone woke her. Brian's voice sounded concerned. "Are you all right, Gram? It's after seven. Aren't you going to eat dinner?"

It took Fonnie a few moments to collect her thoughts. She must have fallen asleep. She looked out the window into the darkness.

Brian's voice came again. "Gram?"

"Yes, yes. I'm fine. I'll be down in just a little bit. I'll meet you in the dining room."

When she arrived, she was pleased to see Stephon sitting with Brian and Tyrone. The three boys, as she now thought of them, seemed to be getting on well together. They were in deep conversation but it looked like a friendly exchange. Good, Fonnie thought, maybe I can erase the nebulous doubts I'd been having about Stephon. If Tyrone likes him, then he must be completely innocent.

"Glad you could join us, Stephon," Fonnie said as she sat down. She looked around the table and said to no one in particular, "Any news?"

All three shook their heads.

Brian said, "Jeremiah had dinner earlier with Clara and Tony. He thought Clara needed family with her. He'll check with you tomorrow."

"That's fine," Fonnie said. "I hope things are going better between her and Tony."

Brian shrugged. "I don't know about that."

Fonnie looked across the table at Stephon. "And how are you feeling now?"

"Like hell. I'm supposed to be back in the office tomorrow," Stephon said, "but I can't leave now. My job be damned, I'm not leaving until Keisha's found."

"We all feel that way," Brian said. "Unfortunately, there's not much we can do right now. Maybe something will come up in the morning."

After the waitress brought their orders, silence settled over the group. Even Tyrone spoke in monosyllables, forsaking his thesaurus vocabulary. Fonnie's concern for Keisha now included her brother. She'd never seen him this distressed.

"Have you called your father yet?" she asked.

Tyrone nodded. "It was hard."

"What did he say?"

"Just told me to pray."

"And that's exactly what you and I are going to do when we finish eating." Fonnie gave him an encouraging smile. "We are going to the Shepherd by the Sea Chapel and have our own prayer meeting."

After last cups of coffee, they walked the short distance to the chapel. The evening was silent, they were silent. Fonnie led the way up the sidewalk to the front. An outdoor light bathed the Shepherd in a soft glow. She could have sworn His smile was a little bigger than it had been the last time she was here.

"Are you sure the church is unlocked," Tyrone asked.

"The caretaker told me it was always left open to the public except when needed for special occasions. Try the door."

Tyrone climbed the steps, opened the door, and stepped in. Fonnie came up behind him and felt along the wall for the light switch. Lights on either side of the aisles lit up the empty pews of the small chapel. They looked warm and welcoming. They were accustomed to giving comfort to the fearful, the troubled, Fonnie thought, to those who had nowhere else to turn.

Fonnie walked slowly toward the altar and sank down in a front row seat. Tyrone sat beside her. The old woman and the young boy both bowed their heads, beseeching the same God in their separate ways.

After several minutes Fonnie heard Tyrone stir. He turned to her and whispered. "Do you think it would be all right if I played the piano? I play for Pop at our church and the music makes me feel closer to God."

"Of course it would be all right."

Tyrone made his way to the piano that sat near the pulpit. He ran his fingers over the keys and presently started playing a quiet hymn. Fonnie watched in fascination as Tyrone sat with his eyes closed and played one prayerful hymn after another. She recognized *Does Jesus Care?* and *All Through the Night*. Some were not familiar to her, but it didn't matter. The music broke the cords of tension that had been twisted tightly around her heart. She took a deep breath, felt a wonderful calmness.

# TWENTY-THREE

KEISHA DIDN'T KNOW how long she'd sat there holding Melanie's hand, or how long she'd cried. It was long enough for her tiny bit of daylight to disappear, and long enough so that when she tried to stand, she stumbled and nearly fell again. She put her hand to her head to still the spinning. Her forehead was fiery hot. Of course she was running a fever. She was dehydrated. She was injured. And soon she could become disoriented, delirious. Even now, she thought she heard angel music.

She leaned her head against the wall to steady herself, inched back down the wall away from Melanie's body. The angel music was coming from above her head. So Pop was right, she thought, heaven is somewhere up there in the sky.

Her legs bumped into the bench again. She turned around very carefully to sit down. Every movement made her woozy. All she wanted to do now was to lie down and wait for the angels to carry her soul away.

But something in her mind jerked her back. She'd always pictured angels as playing harps, not the piano. What she was hearing was definitely a piano. Her brain took a couple more spins around the universe before it slowed down enough for her to realize that perhaps what she was hearing was human music. Maybe help was nearby. She had to get the piano player's attention. But how could she? She couldn't call out. There was nothing she could use to make a noise. Even in her fevered mind, she knew pounding her fist against the cement wall would not be heard above the piano notes. There was nothing she could do.

Keisha slumped back. She wanted to cry again, but there were no tears left. There was only the pain in her throat and the fog trapping her mind. Somewhere in the midst of that fog she heard a line from one of her father's sermons, *I have set before thee an open door.* But, her brain argued back, there is no door except to the bathroom. What good is that? Then she remembered how, when she'd first entered the bathroom, the door had slammed against the wall with a loud bang. Maybe that's what her father was trying to tell her.

She fumbled her way back along the bench until she felt the door sill. The door was open as she had left it after her failed attempt to get a drink of water. She stood up, felt the door to her left, and pushed against it. It hit the wall beside the commode with a dull thud. Not good enough, she thought. She pulled the door toward her and shoved with all her might. She was rewarded with a resounding echo.

But when the door left her hands, she toppled backwards and ended up in a heap on the floor. That was all right. The door had bounced back and made contact with her shoes. Keisha scrunched up, her back and hands flat on the floor, her knees drawn up to her belly, the bottom of her shoes touching the door. With the force of a catapult she thrust her knees forward and her feet drove the door into the wall. To *her* ears it sounded like a cannon shot. Surely the piano player would hear it. Again the door bounced back and again she shot it forward. Again and again. Bang! Bang! BANG!

Keisha's world had been reduced to her thrusting knees and the crashing noise. Her mind no longer functioned.

Fonnie felt a disruption in the calm feeling that had begun to wrap around her. Something alien had crept into the chapel—a noise that didn't fit alongside the peaceful music. She wished whoever was doing that blasted pounding would quit. Tyrone hadn't seemed to have noticed. His eyes were shut and his hands slid softly across the keys. She didn't know the tune, but it was plaintive, sad, a prayer for help.

The song came to an end, and before Tyrone had a chance to start another one, a sound louder than before echoed into the chapel. He jerked up, opened his eyes, scanned the room. "What was that?"

"Some fool pounding on something," Fonnie said. "I don't know where it's coming from, maybe from the street. Sorry it interrupted your playing."

"I guess we'd better be getting back to the motel anyway." Tyrone got up from the piano bench and stepped down off the platform. He and Fonnie made their way to the door. "It's been a long day. Maybe I can get some sleep tonight." He opened the door and held it as Fonnie went out. "You go ahead, I'll switch off the lights."

At that moment another bang resonated from somewhere. Fonnie looked around outside. "I don't see anybody out here. That's strange. What could be making that noise?" She stepped back inside the chapel and looked all around.

"It might be something malfunctioning," Tyrone said. "A furnace perhaps. Does this church have a basement?"

"I don't know," Fonnie said. She turned and stared toward the front of the chapel. "Yes," she said. "I remember now. The caretaker told me about the hurricane room. There's a trap door under the pulpit. "Do you think maybe an animal got in there somehow and got trapped?"

"I don't know what kind of animals there might be skulking around the beach," Tyrone said, "but maybe we'd better report the noise to the caretaker."

"Good idea. I'm sure the desk clerk will know how to reach...." Her sentence was left unfinished as another and louder boom came crashing over the pews. "On the other hand, maybe we'd better have a look ourselves."

Tyrone nodded his head in agreement. He turned and reached the pulpit in two long strides. "The trap door is under here?"

Fonnie hurried behind him as fast as she could. "That's what the caretaker said."

Tyrone gave the pulpit a push that nearly sent it over the edge of the podium. In the floor was a square outline with an inverted handhold. Tyrone grasped the latch. "Well, here it goes." He jerked the door upward and a large opening appeared at his feet. "Like opening the lid of a cigar box," he said. He pushed the lid all the way back, and it dropped open with a loud thump. The noise mingled with another bang from below.

Tyrone bent down and peered into the darkness. "I

don't see anything. Wish I had a flashlight." Another bang. "There's steps here," he said to Fonnie. "I'm going down."

"There has to be a light switch somewhere for the basement. I'll see if I can find it." Fonnie made her way to the far wall as Tyrone started his descent. In a few moments she found some switches and turned them all on. Bright lights accented the choir loft, a baptismal font, and then Fonnie could see light coming up through the trap door.

She hurried back to the door and leaned over. The banging had stopped. "I'm coming down," she yelled.

"No." Tyrone's command stopped her. "Don't come down. I'm calling 911." Fonnie drew back and listened as Tyrone spoke into his cell phone. "I need two ambulances at the Shepherd by the Sea Chapel." His voice choked as he added, "I've found the missing women."

Fonnie heart nearly stopped beating. She crept down two steps until she could see Tyrone. He was cradling Keisha in his arms, his face smeared with tears and blood. "Is she alive?" Fonnie managed to ask.

"Yes. Barely. I don't know about the other one."

She swayed backward with a wave of thankfulness. That's all she needed to know at the moment. Keisha was found, and she was alive. Fonnie called down to Tyrone. "I'll go outside and direct the ambulances."

# TWENTY-FOUR

POLICE CARS ARRIVED with the ambulances. Fonnie paid them scant attention. Her focus was on her friend being carried out on a stretcher. She crowded close to be sure Keisha was breathing. Her mind, her heart kept repeating, *Thank you. Thank you.*

She watched as Keisha was placed in the ambulance. Tyrone crawled in beside his sister, and Fonnie managed to whisper to him, "Brian and I will be at the hospital as soon as possible." Tyrone nodded. She could tell he was too overwhelmed to say anything.

For a moment she wondered why Melanie wasn't being brought up also, but then she knew the answer. Melanie was dead, and the police would examine the scene before moving the body.

Lieutenant Steinberg exited the basement and came up to Fonnie "I called Brian and filled him in. He'd given me his cell phone number earlier. He's coming over to get you."

"Thank you," Fonnie said. "I must get to the hospital—be near Keisha."

"Of course, but I need a statement from you first. How did you and the boy happen to be here?"

"We were led here. The Shepherd led us here."

Steinberg paused. He smiled. "Suppose we have a seat and you take me through it step by step."

She'd barely started when Brian and Stephon came racing in. Brian tried to hug her and toss questions at her simultaneously while Stephon kept trying to say something between wiping tears from his cheeks. The detective gave a time-out signal and ushered them into a pew. "Now the sooner I get the facts, the sooner you all can get to the hospital."

THE EMERGENCY ROOM waiting area was empty except for Tyrone and two uniformed policemen. Stephon rushed over to Tyrone, scooted down beside him. Tyrone looked at him with bloodshot eyes. "She's bad off. She's really bad off."

Stephon clenched his hands. "When I get my hands on the bastard who did this…." His voice broke. He took a deep breath. "Does she know who it was? Can she tell the police anything?"

Tyrone shook his head. "I don't know. She was out of her head when I found her. She may not know anything."

Brian went over to talk to the cops. Fonnie found a bathroom, got some wet paper towels and used them to wipe smudges of blood off Tyrone's face. He smiled his appreciation.

"Have you called your father?" she asked.

"Yes. A deacon in our church is driving him up in the morning. For tonight he's continuing the prayer meeting. Now it'll be prayers of thanksgiving along with petitions for her recovery."

"Like Jeremiah said, 'prayer is a powerful force', and our finding Keisha is proof of that."

There was little else to say as the small group kept their vigil. Other patients with minor injuries trickled in and out, bandaged or limping or rolled in wheelchairs. Lieutenant Steinberg showed up, but the policemen shook their heads when he inquired about developments. It seemed hours before a doctor came out to give them news about Keisha.

"Miss Rigg's condition is critical, but we've stabilized her and she's being taken to ICU. She has injuries to her larynx and her esophagus due to attempted strangulation. Her trachea escaped major damage, but if the edema or the swelling in her throat increases, we may have to do a tracheotomy."

Tyrone stood up to face the doctor. "But she'll make it? She's going to be all right?"

"She has a long road ahead of her, and it's too soon to know the outcome."

"Is she conscious?" Stephon asked. "Does she know where she is?"

"She's sedated now and will stay that way for awhile. Then we'll see." The doctor turned to the police at the other side of the room. "I have to talk to the police now. You can go up to the ICU waiting room—third floor. The nurse there will let you know when you can see Miss Riggs."

Tyrone and Stephon headed for the elevator. Fonnie hesitated and looked over to Brian. He motioned her to go ahead. She was glad that Brian was getting along so well with the local police. It meant he would be privy to whatever information they had and he could tell her later.

They hadn't been upstairs long when Jeremiah

came in. "Sorry I didn't get here sooner," Jeremiah said to Fonnie. "But I felt I had to stay with Hank and Doris for a while. Hank's pretty torn up about Melanie."

"I can imagine. I'm sure he was holding out hope that she would be found alive and well. And now this—this horrible ending." Fonnie knew that horrible was a feeble word to describe what had happened to Melanie and to the torture that Keisha had suffered, but it was all her brain could come up with at the moment. "Did the police tell him time of death or anything definite?"

"No. That will have to wait for the autopsy." Jeremiah shifted in his chair. "Any sign of Keisha coming around?"

"I don't know. They haven't let anyone in to see her yet."

"They're not likely to, either." Jeremiah stared across the room at an officer in a straight-back chair tipped back against the wall. "No one is going to get by him without police clearance. Thank God for that."

"It seems so unreal," Fonnie said. "There's a person out there who killed Melanie and who tried to kill Keisha."

"A person who now knows he failed with one of his victims," Jeremiah said. "So what does he do now?"

Fonnie shuddered. She looked over at Stephon, his head buried in his hands—big, strong hands. Her gaze returned to Jeremiah. "I don't know," she said. "What does he do now?"

If Jeremiah had an answer, he didn't have a chance to give it because two more visitors entered the waiting room. Fonnie welcomed Clara and Lula with a faint smile.

Clara ran over and gave Fonnie a hug. "How is she?"

"The doctor says she's critical but stable. That's all we know." Fonnie squeezed Clara back. "I appreciate you coming, youngun, but you need to be in bed. You've got to take care of that great-grandbaby of mine."

Clara brushed back tears. "I'm so glad Dad married Amy. It's been hard with my mother and both grandmothers gone. Now I have a stepmother and a step-grandmother, all at one time."

Lula stepped forward. "Actually you should be in bed also, Fonnie. Keisha is going to need you tomorrow when she wakes up. Let me take you back so you can get some rest." Fonnie was surprised that Lula looked and sounded stone sober.

Her eyes were red-rimmed but they were clear and steady. Her voice was firm, kindly. Her words made sense.

Jeremiah spoke up in agreement. "She's right. In fact, you all need to be at your best in the morning. There may be some major developments."

"But what about Tyrone. I'm sure he won't leave and someone needs to stay with him."

Lula looked over at the two young men slumped in their seats. "I doubt that Stephon will budge tonight and Edgar said he was coming over later to check on Keisha."

"Tony's coming too," Clara said. "He wanted to be sure Hank and Doris were all right before he left. But Midge said she would stay with them as long as she was needed."

"Brian and I will be here too for Tyrone," Jeremiah said. "So you three run along." He stood up and put an arm around Lula's shoulders. "I'm trusting you to take care of my girls."

Lula looked startled. Fonnie thought that it had probably been a long time since anyone had put their trust in Lula.

# TWENTY-FIVE

FONNIE AWOKE AT SEVEN, surprised that she had slept so long and so well. Her first thought was to phone the hospital and get a report on Keisha. On second thought she decided to call Brian on his cell. He was probably still at the hospital and could tell her what was happening.

He answered on the first ring. "Tyrone, Stephon, and I took turns sleeping on the one decent couch in the waiting room," Brian said. "Edgar and Tony only stayed a few minutes, once they found out Keisha was still out of it, and that they wouldn't be allowed to see her. I sent Jeremiah back to the motel to get some sleep. He said he'd have breakfast with you and bring you back over."

"Good. You didn't get to see Keisha at all?"

"I didn't, but the nurse let Tyrone in for a few minutes early this morning. Keisha had opened her eyes and the nurse thought she might recognize her brother."

"Did she?"

"Tyrone said he wasn't sure. She just gave him a blank stare, but when he spoke to her, she seemed to become more alert, and he thought she tried to smile. Then she closed her eyes and drifted off again."

"They'd better let me in to see her," Fonnie said. "You can bet your bottom dollar she'll recognize my voice."

Brain laughed. "I'll admit it's pretty hard to ignore you. You have a special talent for getting to people."

"I'll take that as a compliment," Fonnie said. "Now what are your plans for the day?"

"I'm hanging out here until the doctor makes his rounds, which should be soon. Then I'm hauling my buddies over to the motel and three of us are heading for showers and food—in that order."

"Fine. But don't leave until I get there."

FONNIE AND JEREMIAH arrived as the doctor in his starched white lab coat and Lieutenant Steinberg in his rumpled brown suit came through the ICU double doors. The three disheveled young men hurried to meet them, as did the two older people. Steinberg motioned all of them into a far corner.

The doctor spoke first. His report was succinct and professional. "Miss Riggs' condition has been upgraded from critical to serious. She is aware and as alert as possible with the pain medication she requires. The edema in her throat is subsiding. At the present time she is unable to talk or swallow. These functions may well return in a few days. She is being fed intravenously and receiving the necessary antibiotics and analgesics." The doctor smiled at the attentive group in front of him. "I'll check her again at noon and give you an update at that time. Are there any questions?"

Of course there were. Tyrone was first. "Sir, I have to call our dad and give him a report. He was planning on coming here this morning, but I talked to him a few minutes ago and he didn't sound good. He has a bad heart and I urged him to stay home until he heard from me. Can I tell him that Keisha's going to be all right?"

"I think that would be a safe statement. However, I do have to caution you that she may have residual cognitive problems and memory deficit, especially if her brain was deprived of oxygen for any length of time."

Tyrone flinched. "You mean, she might have mental problems."

"Perhaps. I'm not saying she will, but I have to give you the possibilities. You understand?"

Tyrone nodded his head, wiped his hand across his dry lips. "Yes sir. Thank you."

Stephon stepped in front of the group. His voice was harsh as he asked, "When can I see her?"

"As far as I'm concerned, Miss Riggs can have visitors according to the ICU policy, but since this is also a police case, I'm leaving that up to Lieutenant Steinberg." He turned, nodded to the detective and the assemblage, and left the room.

Stephon put both hands on his hips and stared defiantly at the detective. "Well? Can I see her now?"

Steinberg shook his head. "Fraid not, son. I've decided it would be in Miss Riggs' best interest to allow only two visitors. The two would be her brother and Mrs. Beachum."

"What's the big idea? I'm a good friend. I have a right to see her."

The detective's voice became hard, but he gave Stephon a smile. "You'll be able to see her when I think it's safe. I'll let you know."

Tyrone took Stephon's arm and pulled him aside. "It's okay, Bro. They know what's best. I'll tell Keisha you've been waiting out here all night, and that you'll see her soon."

"Sure. Fine."

Fonnie's thoughts were in turmoil. She was delighted she was going to be allowed to see Keisha, but she was disturbed by Stephon's attitude. Was it the natural result of his anxiety and fatigue? And why was Lieutenant Steinberg refusing to allow him and others in to see Keisha?

Fonnie had several questions she wanted to ask, but wasn't sure now was an appropriate time. She was glad when Brian spoke up. "Sir, the doctor said Keisha couldn't talk, but is she able to communicate in other ways—in writing or body language?"

"She apparently understands simple questions and can give positive or negative responses. That's as far as we've gone so far."

Fonnie felt someone bump her elbow and she turned to see a young woman with a camera in her hand. The woman waved to get the detective's attention and shouted out her question. "Does she know who did this to her?"

Steinberg glared at the interloper. "This is no place for reporters. If you will be at the police station at nine o'clock, I'll have a statement for the press then."

The young woman shrugged and said to no one in particular, "You can't blame a gal for trying." She slung her camera over her arm and turned her back. Several pairs of eyes shot daggers at her as she left.

The gal was definitely out of order, Fonnie thought, but she had voiced the question everyone was probably wondering.

After Lieutenant Steinberg left, Fonnie approached the nurse and asked when she and Tyrone would be allowed to visit. "It'll be at least an hour," the nurse said. She's due for respiratory therapy and other treatments. I'll come get you."

"You boys might better go get cleaned up and get some breakfast," Fonnie said to Brian and Tyrone. "Jeremiah and I will man the fort while you're gone."

"I may not be back this morning," Brian said. "I've got to spend some time with Hank. I haven't even had a chance to talk to him about the arrangements for Melanie." He blinked back tears. "You know, Gram. I really did like her."

Fonnie couldn't say anything. She hoped Brian would never hear all the derogatory comments that had made the rounds about Melanie's reputation. Maybe he could remember her as a sweet beautiful girl.

"Stephon and I will be back as soon as we can," Tyrone said to Fonnie. "Stephon wants to be here even if he can't see her."

"I understand."

Fonnie turned to Jeremiah who had been standing quietly by her side for the past several minutes. "You're awfully quiet this morning. A penny for your thoughts."

"I've been watching and listening. Let's find some comfortable chairs and compare notes."

They settled themselves close to the ICU door where they could see the police officer on duty. "I wonder how long they'll keep a guard here," Fonnie said.

"As long as necessary. As long as there's a killer on the loose." Jeremiah leaned back and crossed one leg over the over. "Which brings up one point I'm concerned about. Why is Stephon barred from seeing Keisha? Reckon the police regard him as a suspect?"

"Of course not. Remember, they've barred everyone except Tyrone and me. And that includes you and Brian. They simply want to be sure she's not overwhelmed with visitors. Makes sense to me."

"I guess so. But what about this business of her not being able to talk? You think that's for real? Or is it some kind of cover?"

"I don't know why the doctor would mislead us on that. At any rate, I'll find out when they let me in. I hope it's soon."

The wait was less than an hour. Fonnie was on her second cup of coffee when the nurse came up to her and led her through the double doors. There'd been many changes in hospitals and especially in intensive care units since she'd done active nursing. One thing never changed though, and that was the permeating odor of antiseptics. Fonnie inhaled deeply of the remembered scent. It brought a measure of comfort. Keisha was where she needed to be, was receiving the best of care.

Fonnie approached the bed warily, not knowing exactly what to expect. Her last view of Keisha had been on a gurney being wheeled into an ambulance, her face streaked with blood, her breathing barely perceptible. She lay now with her head slightly elevated, her hair combed neatly, a small bandage over her left eye, her hospital gown pulled high up on her neck, and oxygen tubing in her nostrils. Her eyes were partially open, and she had a peaceful look on her face.

"Good morning, Keisha," Fonnie said softly. She

went over to the side of the bed opposite the IV pole. "You look good."

Keisha's lips curved slightly upward, her hand went to her throat.

"That's all right," Fonnie said. "You needn't try to talk. I'll just sit with you a little." She pulled up a straight back chair and placed it within Keisha's line of vision. "Tyrone's gone back to the motel to take a shower. He was here all night and will be back shortly." Again Keisha looked as if she wanted to smile, but couldn't quite make her lips follow her command. Her eyelids fluttered, popped open, and then closed again.

The nurse came over. "I had to give her more morphine after her respiratory therapy. She'll sleep for a while now."

Fonnie gave Keisha's hand a pat, and backed away. The nurse walked with her to the door. "She's doing well. She's going to be fine."

"Has she said anything at all?"

"No. She wants to, but the swelling is still too much. We're giving her medication for it. She might be able to talk by tomorrow."

"Do you think she remembers what happened?"

"Up to a point. She was able to demonstrate to the police how she was grabbed from behind and choked. But when asked if she saw her attacker's face or knew who it was, she indicated she didn't. She doesn't seem to remember being rescued or who rescued her."

"Did she know her brother when he came in last night?"

The nurse shrugged. "I wasn't on duty then. The night nurse didn't comment on it, so I don't know."

"Thanks," Fonnie said. "Tyrone, her brother, should be back soon. Can he come in then?"

"Of course. Have him knock on the door when he gets here."

A short while later Tyrone and Stephon came back looking once again like respectable young men.

"Anything new?" Stephon asked.

"I saw her for a few minutes," Fonnie said. "She looks good. She tried to smile, then she went back to sleep." Fonnie turned to Tyrone. "The nurse said you could go in when you got back."

"Great. Oh, I called Pop again," Tyrone said. "Since Keisha is doing well now, I talked him into staying home. He agreed he was too tired to travel, but he said he was scheduling a victory celebration at the church for tonight. They'll be praising the Lord so loud we'll probably be able to hear them way up here."

"Your pop has the right idea," Jeremiah said. "I wish we could have a celebration of our own at the Shepherd's Chapel, but it hardly seems appropriate, with Hank planning Melanie's funeral."

"I know," Tyrone said. "I wish it could have been a happy ending for everyone. Brian's having a rough time. On the way up here he kept telling me how beautiful Melanie was."

Stephon rubbed the back of his neck. "Melanie had outward beauty, that's for sure, but she couldn't hold a candle to Keisha when it came to inward beauty." He let out a deep sigh. "Oh God, why won't they let me see her? I'm going crazy."

"Hang in there," Jeremiah said. "They won't let me in either, you know. But maybe the police will have a change of heart later today." He steered Stephon over to a seat. "Come on, we just have to wait it out."

Tyrone knocked on the ICU door and was let in. Fonnie pretended interest in a *Woman's Day* magazine while Jeremiah sipped coffee and Stephon paced.

In a few minutes Tyrone came stumbling out, tears streaming down his face. He collapsed in a chair and moaned.

# TWENTY-SIX

FONNIE STARED AT TYRONE in alarm. Stephon tore to his side. "What? What happened?"

"She fought me. She hit me." Tyrone choked on a huge sob. "She didn't want me to be near her." He swiped angrily at his eyes. "The nurse said I upset Keisha and that I had to leave. But I didn't do anything to upset her. It's like she just went crazy all of a sudden."

"I don't understand," Fonnie said. "What did you say to her?"

"Nothing. That is, I told her she looked great and that she'd soon be able to go home. She had her eyes half closed, but I'm sure she recognized me, knew my voice. Then she went berserk, scratching and clawing at me. She tried to cry out, but could only make a rattling noise. I backed away and tried to reason with her. That's when the nurse came running up and chased me out."

"That doesn't make sense," Stephon said. "You must have said something to set her off."

Tyrone shook his head violently. "I tell you I didn't! I don't know what happened."

"Maybe I know," Jeremiah said. Three puzzled faces turned toward the old man. "She may have had a flashback as in post-traumatic syndrome. After all, she's been through her own private war. You may have triggered something that put her back in the midst of her battle. She wasn't fighting you, Tyrone. She was fighting her attacker."

"Yes. That must be the explanation," Fonnie said. "If only we knew what the trigger had been. You have to tell Lieutenant Steinberg about it. Tell him everything."

STEINBERG, HOWEVER, did not return to the hospital that morning to hear about Keisha's flashback. He was busy conferring with Midge Garrison and others at the motel about Buzz's autopsy results.

Brian was on the scene when the grim-faced detective came into the motel looking for Midge. He found her on the verandah surrounded by everyone there who had been in the wedding party except those keeping watch at the hospital.

Later Brian reported the happenings to the hospital watch team just as they unfolded.

Lieutenant Steinberg slumped down in a vacant chair, motioned everyone to stay. "All of you might as well hear this. We have received Mr. Garrison's autopsy report. His death was the result of a massive overdose of Clonidine, a medication used for high blood pressure, also known as Catapres." He raised his hand to forestall questions and comments. "One symptom of an overdose could be nausea. A massive overdose would result in dyspnea or difficult breathing, a slowing of the heart rate, and finally heart failure. Its effects are increased when taken with alcohol. It comes in tablet form, but could have been crushed and added to his food or beverage. Mr. Garrison's death is now being considered a homicide."

The ensuing silence was broken by a series of sobs from Midge as she clutched the arms of her chair. There were gasps from others as they stared at the detective. It was a few moments before anyone spoke, then Edgar's forceful voice asked, "But couldn't it have been an accident? Maybe he took extra blood pressure medicine on his own."

Midge shook her head wildly. "My Buzz didn't take blood pressure medicine. His blood pressure was fine." She dabbed at her eyes and wadded the tissue into a tight ball. "But who would want to kill Buzz?"

"Our investigation is just beginning. We'll find the answer in time. Right now it seems that he may have been given some of the drug in the days before the wedding, which would account for his flu symptoms. Then a massive dose was administered in a drink at the reception, causing him to collapse."

Clara sat forward in her chair, stared hard at Steinberg. "If the poisoning started before he arrived here, then it had to be someone who was with him in Florida. Is that right, Lieutenant?"

"If that's the case."

Clara leaned back with a look of relief on her face, and Brian noticed she flashed a big smile at Tony. Tony was studying the floor.

"But you don't know for a fact," Hank said, "that the poisoning started in Florida. Do you?"

Steinberg didn't answer the question. "What we do know for a fact is that we have the glass he drank from at the reception and it has traces of Clonidine in it."

"Isn't that interesting?" Lula said. "And where did you find that?"

Again the detective didn't answer. He turned to Midge. "As I said before, our investigation is just beginning. However, the body is being released for burial and you can make your arrangements."

"You mean we can take him home now?"

Steinberg nodded. "I'm sorry for the delay. You understand the local medical examiner held the body as a precautionary measure since he couldn't determine the cause of death."

Midge fished in her pocket for another tissue, swiped at her tears. "Of course. I understand."

Edgar came over and put his arm around her. "You go on to your room now and rest. I'll take care of everything."

"Thank you. It's such a comfort to have you here."

Doris rose and went over to Midge. "I'll go up with you, help you start packing."

Hank waited until Midge and Doris had gone into the lobby, then he scooted his chair closer to Steinberg. "What about Melanie?" His voice cracked. "Can I take her home too? I'm the only family she had left. Her parents are buried in an old family cemetery near Richmond. That's where I'll put her to rest." He caught his breath. "Poor sweet Melanie."

"I'll let you know. We should have her autopsy results soon."

Steinberg rose to leave, but Hank had one more question. "You think the same guy is responsible?"

"It's too early to comment on that."

Brian followed Steinberg as he strode through the lobby. The detective turned to him. "How's your grandmother holding up under the strain?"

"Fairly well. She's putting up a good front, but she's really worried about Keisha."

"We all are. It's a miracle Miss Riggs survived, and we're going to make sure nothing else happens to her. Are you going to the hospital now?"

"Yes sir. I'll tell Gram you were asking about her." Brian hesitated. "But I'd like to ask you a question if I may."

"Sure. What is that?"

"The glass you said you found that Buzz drank from—that contained the drug—was that the fragment of a glass you found in Keisha's room?"

"That it was. Contrary to popular opinion, we were not ignoring Garrison's death. We had his fingerprints and so when we found the glass, we checked it out. Had his prints on it as well as several others, probably kitchen staff, but we're still making comparisons. Finding the glass in Miss Rigg's room brought up several questions. Was Miss Riggs suspicious of somebody and so saved the piece of glass? Did she see someone messing with Buzz's drink? If she was suspicious, why didn't she tell the police immediately? And lastly, was she trying to blackmail someone and almost got herself killed as a result?"

"The answers to the first three questions," Brian said, "are 'I don't know' but I do know she isn't a blackmailer."

Steinberg pushed the front door open, made for his car. "I'll be at the hospital later. Maybe Miss Riggs will be able to give us the answers herself."

# TWENTY-SEVEN

WHEN BRIAN FINISHED giving Steinberg's report to the four at the hospital, Fonnie was the first to respond. "I knew it. I knew there was a connection between Buzz's death and the disappearances."

"But we still don't know why," Jeremiah said, "or who."

"What's this about Florida?" Tyrone asked. "You didn't tell me that part of it, Brian."

"All I know is that Buzz complained of being sick before he got to the wedding, so it must have started when they were in Miami."

Fonnie noticed that Stephon had listened to Brian's account without comment. Maybe it's time he did make a comment, she thought. He must have an opinion about the poisoning. "Suppose you tell us what you think, Stephon," Fonnie said. "You were in Miami when Buzz first got sick."

Brian whirled around, stared at Stephon. "You were in Miami? With Buzz? With Melanie? Why didn't I know this?"

Stephon backed further into the corner of his chair. "I was just there to see a Miami Heat game. And I thought I'd look in on Buzz and Hank. I'd played golf with them at home. Melanie happened to be there that same night. That's all."

"And Buzz was sick then?" Brian said.

"We all went out to dinner and Buzz was fine. The next day when I stopped by before heading home, he was a little under the weather. I didn't think anything about it."

"Never mind that," Jeremiah said. "Let's get back to the matter at hand. Brian, did you say Steinberg was planning on trying to get more information from Keisha?"

Brian nodded. "How is she doing now, Gram? More aware of things?"

"Much more, now that they've been able to ease up on her pain medication. She's more comfortable and is able to take sips of water. The doctor doesn't want her to try to talk yet. Tyrone did have a scary moment with her this morning, though."

"What happened?"

Tyrone told him of Keisha's apparent flashback and of her fighting against him. "I don't know what set her off."

"Try to remember exactly what you did," Brian said. "Did you make some sudden movement? Something that she could have interpreted as being a threat?"

"Nothing I can think of. I was talking to her, then I leaned forward, and I think my hand may have rubbed her arm. That's when she went berserk and the nurse came over and sent me out. It was terrible."

"But she's all right now," Fonnie said. "Tyrone and I went in together about an hour ago. She was sitting up. She knew us right away and even motioned Tyrone to come close and she kissed him on the cheek."

"I asked her if she remembered me coming in earlier and she shook her head no. But then she rubbed her neck as if it still hurt to move. One of the nurses brought her a pencil and a clip board with paper and suggested she write her answers to us."

"Great idea," Brian said. "Was she able to do that? Did you ask her anything else?"

"I didn't want to upset her so I kept my questions light. Like, what was the first thing she wanted to eat when she was able? She quickly wrote *ice cream,* just as I expected. Then she added *strawberry*. That's always been her favorite."

"Then she had a question of her own," Fonnie said. "She wrote in capital letters *STEPHON*? So we assured her that he had been here all the time and would be able to see her soon."

Brian gave Stephon a quick smile then turned back to Tyrone. "But you didn't ask what she remembered about her attack or attacker?

Tyrone shook his head. "I thought that ought to be left up to the police. Fonnie did ask her if she liked my piano playing." He grinned at Fonnie. "I guess that was her way of finding out if Keisha remembered anything about her rescue last night."

"And?"

"She wrote *adagio*."

Brian frowned. "What does that mean? I never studied music."

"Adagio is a slow tempo," Tyrone said. "She thought my playing was too slow. And it was. I didn't feel like playing anything lively. But the important thing is she remembered it, so chances are, she remembers other things also. She may have a lot to tell the police when they get here."

"Good," Brian said. "I'm going to call Steinberg right now. Hopefully he can get here soon."

Lieutenant Steinberg arrived a few minutes later. He conferred with the nurse on duty before coming over to the waiting group. "The nurse says it will be all right for me to question Miss Riggs now. I'm taking the officer on duty here in with me as a witness and I would also like Mrs. Beachum to accompany us."

"Me?" Fonnie was both surprised and flattered. "Sure. Be glad to do anything I can to help." She pushed forward in her chair and made an ineffectual attempt to stand. "Help me up, Tyrone, please. I've been sitting here so long I've gotten stiff."

Tyrone hurried to her side. "I'm always enraptured to facilitate your mobility."

Fonnie laughed. "Cut the big words and just get me on my feet."

"At your service, Madame." He reached down, took her hands in his and pulled her up.

"Thanks, but you need some lotion on those rough hands of yours." Fonnie reached into her purse and handed him a tube of hand cream. "Try this. It'll make your hands as smooth as a magnolia blossom."

Tyrone took the proffered cream. "I'll try anything, but hard work is bound to show through."

Fonnie turned her attention to the detective. "Ready when you are."

Lieutenant Steinberg stepped back and motioned Fonnie to go ahead. The nurse met them at the door. "She's doing really well now, but don't tire her."

"We won't stay long," Steinberg assured her.

When they approached the bed, Keisha smiled at

Fonnie and waved her fingers in greeting. She gave the two men a cautious look. "This is Lieutenant Steinberg," Fonnie said. "He was here earlier. Remember?"

Keisha tipped her head slightly. Fonnie went on, "He wants to ask you some questions. It's very important. You can write your answers on the paper like you did to Tyrone and me. Okay?" Again Keisha nodded.

Lieutenant Steinberg slid a chair close to the bed and sat down. He motioned for the officer to pull up another chair. "Miss Riggs, we are going to be taking a formal statement from you. We will be recording my questions to you, and Sergeant Hayes here will be a witness to what you write on your tablet and will read it aloud. Do you understand?"

Keisha reached for her clipboard and wrote *Yes.*

"Good. Mrs. Beachum will be sitting on the other side of the bed to be sure we don't stay too long. First, I want to go over some facts with you." Steinberg shifted to a more comfortable position. "Did you know Melanie Peacock was found dead in the same room where you were held?"

*Yes. I found her. I knew she was dead.*

As Keisha finished writing each answer, Sergeant Hayes read it aloud so it could be audibly recorded.

Steinberg went on, "She was strangled just as you were strangled. You apparently put up more of a fight than she did and that saved your life. Do you remember your attack?"

*Yes. He grabbed me from behind. Covered my mouth. Choked me. I kicked at him. Tried to get away.*

"Are you sure it was a man?"

Keisha thought a moment, nodded. *Tall. Strong. Must have been man.*

"Did he have any kind of odor? Aftershave or anything?"

*Not that I remember.*

"Do you think you kicked him hard enough to leave a bruise?"

*Probably not. Wearing sneakers.*

"Where did the attack happen?"

*In the stairwell. It was dark.*

"Did you see him at all?"

*No.*

"Did he say anything?"

*No.*

"Do you know why he tried to kill you?"

Keisha hesitated then wrote slowly. *The paper.*

"What paper?"

*Paper from Buzz's pocket. I took it. Put in my pocket. It's gone.*

"What was on the paper?"

*Names. Questions. Didn't understand it.*

"But you thought it might be important and you took it. What did you plan to do with it?

*Don't know. Maybe show it to Fonnie.* Keisha looked over to Fonnie, then wrote, *I was worried about Amy.*

When Sergeant Hayes repeated the answer, Fonnie leaned over the bed. "Why were you worried about her?"

Keisha's face crinkled up. Tears formed in her eyes. *The paper. It may involve Amy.*

Steinberg held up his hand to ward off Fonnie's next comment. "Later I want you to try to duplicate what was on the paper. Can you do that?"

*Yes.*

"Right now let's get back to the attack. Do you remember anything that might help identify who he was?"

*No.* Then she quickly added, *Do* you *know anything?*

"Afraid not. He wore gloves. No identifiable prints on the trap door or anywhere in the basement room except for Tyrone's and for yours. We got both yours and your brother's prints while you were in the emergency room. We needed them for comparison. We found your prints all over the walls."

Keisha's eyes half closed and Fonnie wondered if she was trying to block out the memory of her imprisonment. In a few moments, she looked up and wrote, *I was looking for a door—a way out.*

"I see," Steinberg said. "Unfortunately there was only the trap door above your head."

*Who would know about the trap door?*

"Anybody who ever visited the town. The chapel and its hurricane room are described in a Chamber of Commerce pamphlet that is placed in every motel room and public building. You must have one in your room."

*I didn't read it.*

"About your room. We found a portion of a broken glass there. Where did you get it and why did you keep it?

Keisha leaned back on her pillow and seemed in deep thought. She sat up and started writing, *I don't remem* She sat up straighter, crossed off what she had written and started over. *At reception. It was Buzz's glass that he broke. Janitor missed a piece and I picked it up to throw it away.*

"Why didn't you?"

*I guess I forgot to.*

"You weren't suspicious of it and kept it to show to the police?"

*No. Why would I?*

"Because it had a residue of a drug in it—the same drug that killed Buzz."

Keisha dropped her pencil and stared at the detective in wide-eyed amazement. She gave a gasp, groped her bed linen for the pencil, and wrote hurriedly. *Buzz really poisoned?*

"Yes. In his drink."

*What kind of poison?*

"Not a poison as such. An easily obtainable medication. He was given an overdose of a blood pressure medicine—Clonidine. Apparently the tablets were crushed and the powder dissolved in his drink."

Keisha laid the pencil down again and rubbed her chin and lips. Fonnie recognized this mannerism that Keisha often displayed when she was trying to remember something. Apparently it worked. She grabbed the pencil and starting scribbling. *Melanie had powder in her ring!*

As Sergeant Hayes read the sentence out loud, Steinberg shook his head. "What ring?"

Fonnie answered the question before Keisha had a chance. "Melanie's sterling silver ring that was supposed to hold lip gloss. That's the one you mean, Keisha?"

Keisha nodded slowly.

"Oh Lordy," Steinberg said. "And I just released the body and her personal effects. Excuse me, Miss Riggs, but I've got to stop them. Thanks for your help. Please sign these papers and give them to the officer. I'll get back to you later."

Lieutenant Steinberg was issuing orders into his phone as he ran out. Sergeant Hayes watched Keisha sign her name, collected the papers, and resumed his post at the door.

"Well," Fonnie said. "What do you know about that?"

Keisha started a fresh sheet of paper. *Could the drug have been in Melanie's ring?*

"Sounds awfully far fetched. I don't know what to make of it. Guess we'll just have to wait and see what they find." Fonnie looked at Keisha with concern. "You need to rest now. Try to put everything out of your mind and just rest. I'll send Tyrone in later."

Keisha held up her hand for Fonnie to wait and reached for the clipboard again. *Tell Stephon "Hey" for me.*

"I'll do that. Now rest. That's an order."

KEISHA LAID HER HEAD BACK, closed her eyes, but her mind couldn't rest. She kept going over the detective's questions. One particular question stuck in her head, the one about anything she knew that might help to identify her attacker. There seemed to be a teasing voice telling her there was something she needed to remember. But what was it? She believed she had told the detective everything she could recall. Still there was something—something important. Would she remember it before it was too late?

Keisha couldn't even specify what she meant by too late, but she was afraid that if she didn't remember, something else dreadful might happen.

# TWENTY-EIGHT

WHEN FONNIE CAME OUT of ICU, she was surprised to see Stephon sitting alone in the waiting room. "What happened to your cohorts?" "They went to the cafeteria. Jeremiah was determined that Tyrone eat something. This waiting is really getting him down."

"Looks like it's getting to you too," Fonnie said. "You didn't want to eat?"

"Not now. Not until I know Keisha will recover." He stared at Fonnie with eyes bleary with lack of sleep and worry. "How is she? What went on in there, and why did Steinberg bolt out like he did?"

Fonnie hesitated before answering. She hadn't been told to keep any information confidential, and she would have blurted out everything to Brian and Tyrone, but Stephon was a different matter. She was puzzled by her reservation, and so she did what she had always done in such situations, she went with her gut feeling. "Keisha's making progress," she told him, "but she still is not remembering much. The attack and subsequent events seem to be a blur in her mind. And since she can't talk yet, there's little to be learned."

Fonnie watched Stephon's reaction to her report. Was it her imagination, or did he appear to be relieved? He leaned back in his chair and studied the ceiling for a few moments. Then he sat straight up again. "But Steinberg—what made him dash out?"

The lie formed quickly on Fonnie's lips, "Oh, he got a call about another case. That's all."

Before Stephon could say anything else, Clara and Lula entered the waiting room. "We've come to take you out for some fresh air," Clara said to Fonnie. "And some decent food."

"That's right," Lula said. "No hospital or motel fare. We're heading for *Seafood Heaven,* the best crab, the best shrimp, the best everything within fifty miles."

Fonnie gazed at Lula and then glanced at her watch. It was almost five-thirty and Lula still seemed stone sober. It was a pleasant surprise for Fonnie, and she hoped that *Seafood Heaven* didn't have a liquor license.

"But I can't leave right now," Fonnie said. "I have to wait until Brian and the others get back."

Stephon smiled at her. "No, you don't. I'll tell them where you've gone. You need to take a break."

"All right," Fonnie said as she shoved herself out of her seat. "And you two can catch me up on what's going on in the outside world."

They took the elevator down and were nearly out the door when Fonnie pulled back. "My sweater. I left my sweater in the waiting room. I'd better go back and get it. It gets cool as soon as the sun goes down."

"I'll go with you," Lula said, "while Clara brings the car around."

They entered the waiting room and Fonnie went over to the seats where she and Stephon had been sitting a few minutes earlier. Her sweater was there. Stephon was not. She looked around and was startled to see him entering the ICU door. She grabbed her sweater, slung it over her purse, and hurried across the room as fast as she could.

Lula rushed to her side. "What's going on?"

"That's what I want to know." Fonnie shoved against the door.

A nurse she hadn't seen before stopped her entry. "May I help you?" the nurse asked.

"Where's the man who just came in? He's not supposed to be here."

"Mr. Riggs? He's visiting his sister. I just showed him in."

"That's not Mr. Riggs. Keisha's not his sister. He has no right here." Fonnie pushed past the nurse, darted to Keisha's cubicle. The nurse was right behind her. Lula was right behind the nurse.

Fonnie saw Stephon leaning over Keisha, his hands on her face. Keisha's eyes were wide open, her lips curved upward.

When Fonnie reached the bed, she raised her right arm and flung her purse and sweater into Stephon's face.

He reeled back. "What the hell?" He stared wildly at the determined old woman across the bed. "Are you crazy?"

"Not half as crazy as you are if you think I'm going to let you hurt Keisha anymore." She turned to the nurse. "Get him out of here. Now!"

The nurse took him by the arm. "I'm sorry, Mr. Riggs. You'd better leave until we can get this sorted out."

Lula stepped forward. "That man's name is Stephon Weber, not Riggs. Why did you let him in? And where's the cop that's supposed to be guarding Keisha?"

Stephon shook the nurses' hand off his arm. "I just wanted to see her. I wanted to tell her I loved her. I wasn't going to hurt her, for God's sake." He stalked out of the room. The ICU door slammed behind him.

Fonnie was doing her best to explain to Keisha what had happened. "Don't worry about it. It's only that Stephon didn't have permission to come in. We'll get it straightened out." Keisha gave her a puzzled look, lay back, and shut her eyes.

Fonnie came up to the nurse at the same time Sergeant Hayes reappeared. "Where in the hell have you been?" Fonnie demanded.

The policeman shot his eyebrows up at Fonnie. "In the bathroom. You got a problem with that, ma'am?"

"I'm sure Lieutenant Steinberg will have a problem with it when he finds out you let a possible murderer in to see the patient you're supposed to be guarding."

He faced the nurse. "What is she talking about?"

The nurse shook her head. "You told me that Mrs. Beachum and Mr. Riggs, the patient's brother, were allowed in. Since Miss Riggs was awake, I went to the waiting room to see if her brother wanted to go in. Since that gentleman was the only African-American in the waiting room, I assumed he was Mr. Riggs."

Lula put both her hands on her waist, gave the nurse an incredulous look. "You didn't ask his name?"

"Of course, I did. Well, not really. I called him Mr. Tyrone Riggs and he nodded his head. So why should I have questioned him further?"

Fonnie noticed Sergeant Hayes's face turning a shade paler as he asked, "So an unauthorized person visited the patient?"

"Yes," the nurse said. "I'm sorry, but it wasn't my fault. And nothing happened. Miss Riggs is fine."

"No thanks to you," Lula said. "If Fonnie hadn't whopped him with her purse there's no telling what might have happened. And there's no telling where Stephon might be this very minute."

Sergeant Hayes grabbed his cell phone and punched a number at the same time he tore out to the waiting room. He stopped in mid-stride when he spotted Stephon slumped in a chair.

Lula, Fonnie, and the nurse all stopped and stared too. "How about that?" Lula said. "I thought he'd be halfway to the state line by now."

Fonnie started in Stephon's direction when Lula pulled her back. "The cops can handle this. Let's go. Clara is going to wonder what happened to us."

"No," Fonnie said. "I'm not leaving until I know Keisha's safe. There needs to be two cops here, one to guard Keisha and one to find out what Stephon was up to."

She made her way over to Sergeant Hayes. He gave her a sheepish smile. "I informed Lieutenant Steinberg of the mishap here," he said. "He's on his way. In the meantime, I swear I'll not leave my post. It doesn't look like our friend is going anywhere. Steinberg can question him when he gets here."

Lula gently tugged at Fonnie's arm. "It'll be all right now. Let's go."

AS THEY MADE THEIR WAY to *Seafood Heaven,* Lula gave Clara a blow-by-blow account of the incident.

"Good Lord," Clara said as the story ended, "does

that mean Stephon is the one who attacked Keisha and that he meant to finish the job?"

"Maybe. Maybe not," Clara said from the back seat. "He may simply have taken advantage of the breakdown in security to sneak in to see her. He said he wanted to tell her he loved her. The fact that he didn't run away is in his favor."

Clara looked over at Fonnie. "What do you think?"

"I don't know. I might have over-reacted. Maybe he is innocent. Love can make a person do peculiar things."

"Tell me about it," Lula said. "I've even given up drinking until all this mess is solved. Edgar is so upset about Buzz and Melanie, I decided I had to keep a cool head to look after him. Ain't that love for you?"

Fonnie twisted around in her seat and smiled at Lula. "Sounds like. Edgar's lucky to have you by his side."

*Seafood Heaven* lived up to its name. Fonnie dug into the succulent flounder, the crispy hush puppies, the crunchy coleslaw, and downed several glasses of sugary iced tea. The women kept all talk of murder and misdeeds at bay while they tackled the serious job of eating. At last Lula dropped her fork with a sigh of satisfaction. "I had forgotten how good food could taste."

Clara munched on the last hush puppy. "Just think," she said, "I can claim to be eating for two for the next several months. I'm going to enjoy this pregnancy."

"Enjoy it while you can," Fonnie said. "After the baby comes, you won't have time to eat."

As the waiter cleared away the dishes, their lighthearted chatter faded. Fonnie looked from one young woman to the other. She had become very fond of Clara in the past few days and she was learning to like

Lula more each time they were together. She hoped they both had good futures in front of them. She smiled and tried to block out the foreboding that persisted in the back of her brain.

Clara restarted the conversation. "Tony and I are going home in the morning. We're taking Midge home." She gave a slight shiver. "Buzz's body is on the way to the funeral home now. Hank and Doris will be going later tomorrow. There seems to be some delay about releasing Melanie's body. I don't understand it."

Fonnie didn't actually understand it either, but it had something to do with the powder Keisha had mentioned in Melanie's ring. If the others didn't know about it, though, she wasn't going to tell them. "How horrible that a beautiful wedding ended in two funerals. Your dad and Amy are going to have a terrible homecoming after their honeymoon. All they know at this point is that Buzz died. Jeremiah didn't want to call them about the autopsy result or about Melanie and Keisha."

"I think he made the right decision," Lula said. "There's nothing they could do. When are they returning?"

"Tomorrow night. They're flying back here to get their car, and then they plan on driving home to Virginia on Thursday." Fonnie stirred some more sugar into her tea, took a sip, and then went on. "That's when Keisha and I were planning on going home—after a nice peaceful vacation. Now it looks like she'll be going home in an ambulance. I hope she'll be able to travel soon. She needs to be close to her family, and Tyrone needs to be in school."

"But," Lula said, "will the police let her leave? That is, before they've solved the case?"

Fonnie bristled. "The police have nothing to do with it. It's up to the doctor when she can travel. Besides, she doesn't know a thing about the case."

"She doesn't remember calling you just before she was attacked that night?"

"Calling me?" Fonnie gave Lula a perplexed look. Then all of a sudden, the memory of the story she'd made up came back to her. "Oh, you mean, the call she made when I was half asleep. No, she can't remember making the call, and I can't remember what she said. It may come back to me sometime."

"It probably wasn't important," Clara said. "Our subconscious has a way of blocking out trivial information. The only important thing is that she recovers."

# TWENTY-NINE

IT WAS NEARLY eight o'clock when Clara and Lula left Fonnie at the hospital. They had wanted to take her back to the motel for the night, but Fonnie insisted she had to check on Keisha again. "And I have to find out the aftermath of Stephon's escapade," she said.

She kissed Clara on the cheek. "I probably won't see you again before you leave, so have a good trip home." Turning her head to the back seat, she smiled at Lula. "Hang in there."

When she entered the waiting room, Fonnie was surprised to see only Brian in what she had come to consider the Keisha corner. Another family group occupied chairs in the opposite corner. Brian was thumbing through a copy of *Sports Illustrated,* from back to front, pausing from time to time to scan a picture. He glanced up as she came closer and removed a jacket from the chair next to his. "Have a seat."

"Where are the others?" she asked.

"I sent them back to the motel. Jeremiah looked pretty beat. He's in great condition for a man his age, but he has his limits. And I insisted that Tyrone get away. I told him to run up and down the beach a few times. He's not used to being cooped up."

"Good idea. And Stephon?"

Brian grinned. "Steinberg took care of him. Banned him from the hospital."

"What?"

"Not really. But he quizzed him on his little shenanigan of getting into ICU. Stephon convinced him that it was completely harmless, that he only wanted to see Keisha. So Steinberg let him go, but told him he didn't want to see his face around here again." Brian laughed. "The nurse told me about how you walloped him with your purse. You've got a wicked swing, Gram."

"Oh, dear. I guess I owe him an apology."

"Not at all. You did what any mother hen would do—hit first and ask questions later. He deserved what he got for scaring you like that. Of course, what he did reminds me of some of the stunts you've pulled in the past. You're not above lying to get what you want."

"I know. Maybe I've underestimated that boy. I'm going to have to get better acquainted with him."

Fonnie squirmed around in her chair trying to figure out how to ask her next question without hurting Brian. There was no easy way, so she came out with it. "Did Steinberg tell you about the white powder in Melanie's ring?"

Brian nodded. "He's waiting for it to be identified."

"Do you think she was using cocaine?"

"If she was, I never suspected it. But then, in light of other things I've learned, there was a lot about Melanie's life I never suspected." Brian leaned back in his chair and closed his eyes. Fonnie had to strain to hear his next sentence. "I guess I was a fool for a pretty face."

"We're all fools at one time or another," Fonnie said. "Don't make a habit of it."

Brian sat up straight, forced a smile. "Next time you see me going off the deep end, just zap me with your purse to wake me up."

"Sounds like a plan," Fonnie said. She stood up. "I'm going to ask to see Keisha again and then you can run me back to the motel." She started for the door, then stopped as Lieutenant Steinberg came in their direction. When he got close enough to hear, she said, "I was just going in to see Keisha. Want to come along?"

The detective shot her a bemused look. "That sounds like my line. Are we getting our roles reversed again?"

"Of course not. You boss. Me—spectator."

"Good. Let's keep it that way," he said. "Now, I'm going in to see Miss Riggs. Would you like to come along?"

"Yes, thank you." Fonnie winked at Brian as she and the detective walked past.

Fonnie noticed a different policeman was on guard duty. She hoped Sergeant Hayes hadn't gotten too much of a reprimand for this afternoon's fiasco.

When they reached Keisha's cubicle, Fonnie slipped ahead of the detective and gave her a quick hug. Keisha greeted them with a huge smile. She held up her hand for attention. Steinberg and Fonnie stared expectantly. Keisha opened her mouth, took a deep breath, and said, "A-a-ah." She took another breath and this time she breathed out, "Fon-nie."

Keisha's voice was raspy but it sounded beautiful to Fonnie. "You can talk! How wonderful. Can you eat?"

"Drink." To demonstrate, Keisha reached over to her bedside stand, picked up what looked like a milk-shake and slurped some through a straw.

"Looks like you're well on your way to recovery," Lieutenant Steinberg said. "Has the doctor told you when you could be discharged?"

Keisha nodded. Instead of trying to say anything else, she grabbed the clipboard and wrote, *2-3 days.* Then she added, *ambulance to Groverton hosp.*

"That's great news," Steinberg said.

Fonnie blew her nose and wiped at her eyes. "That's marvelous news."

"And what's your other news?" Steinberg asked. "The officer called me. Said you had something to show me."

Keisha reached under her pillow, pulled out a folded piece of paper and handed it to the detective.

Steinberg unfolded the paper and studied it carefully. "This is what you remember from the paper you found in Buzz's pocket?"

Keisha nodded her head. "Yes," she said. Then she wrote, *It must be important since it was taken.*

"Or it may have fallen from your pocket," the detective said. "It may be insignificant and your attacker may have had no interest in it."

"Taken," Keisha said with raspy force. She grabbed her pencil again and wrote, *Jeans tight, paper would not fall out.*

"She's right," Fonnie said. "Her jeans are so tight I'm surprised she can bend over. I'm afraid she might be cutting off circulation to some vital organs."

Keisha glared at Fonnie and the detective grinned.

"So maybe the paper is significant," Steinberg said.

He examined it more closely. He pointed to where Keisha had printed *Myers, Garrison, Trent Law Firm.* "Does this mean it was on their letterhead?"

"Yes."

"But we don't know for sure that Buzz wrote it. It could have been something he found in the office. And since we don't have the original we can't check the handwriting or fingerprints."

Fonnie scrunched up as close to Steinberg as she dared, trying to get a peek, but he kept it just out of her line of vision. She finally said in exasperation, "Are you going to let me see it or not?"

"Oh," he said, sounding surprised. "Are you interested in this?"

She gave him a withering glance. "I'm doing everything except stand on my head to see it. Of course, I'm interested."

Keisha came out with something that resembled a laugh. "Same—old—Fon—nie."

Steinberg handed Fonnie the paper. "See if you can make anything out of it. But in case it turns out to be a valuable piece of evidence, I don't want any mention of it outside of this room."

"Understood." Fonnie read quickly over the scattered words and names, and noted the many question marks. "Looks like the writer had questions about a lot of things. None of it makes any sense to me." She looked up at Keisha. "When we were here last time, you said you thought Amy might be involved. What made you think that?"

"Trent—stone." She picked up the clipboard and wrote, *Trentstone Estates. Amy's Realty handles their sales.* She watched Fonnie, then wrote, *maybe no connection.*

"There's one way to find out," Fonnie said. "Amy and Paul are flying in tomorrow. We can ask them."

"I'll ask them," Steinberg said. "No need for you to worry about it, Mrs. Beachum."

"Understood," Fonnie repeated. "I appreciate you sharing information with me, and I assure you I'll be discreet."

Lieutenant Steinberg took the paper back, slid it into his pocket, and shook Fonnie's hand. "I'll be going now. What time is your daughter due to arrive?"

"About six. Brian could tell you exactly."

The detective reached across the bed and shook hands with Keisha. "Thanks so much for your help. Have a good night's rest now."

Fonnie's gaze followed Steinberg out of the cubicle. "Nice man. Smart, too. He'll get to the bottom of all this mess. And he's right. You need to rest. Goodnight. I'll see you tomorrow."

Keisha reached out and grasped Fonnie's arm. She waved the clipboard indicating for Fonnie to wait while she wrote another message. The message was short. *Why did you hit Stephon?*

A myriad of answers raced through Fonnie's brain. How could she explain without really explaining? "It was a mistake," she finally said. "I thought he was upsetting you."

Keisha shook her head. Her words came out a little faster than her previous speeches. "He was kissing me."

Fonnie shrugged. "Like I said. It was a mistake. It won't happen again."

"Good."

Fonnie waved good-bye and made a quick exit. The nurse stopped her on the way out. "It won't be necessary for anyone to stay tonight. Miss Riggs is doing well. The doctor has left orders for her to be moved to a regular room in the morning."

"Fine." Fonnie started to push the door, but turned back. "She'll still have a police guard after she's moved, won't she?"

"Oh yes, you can be sure of that."

# THIRTY

FONNIE AWOKE EARLY, refreshed, filled with anticipation and thankfulness. Thankful that Keisha was out of danger and anticipation for the newlyweds' arrival later that day. In the meantime she had high hopes that the good Lieutenant Steinberg would be filling in some of the missing puzzle pieces.

She started going over the missing pieces in her head as she showered and shampooed. But her mind was soon sidetracked to thinking about her hair. It had definitely taken a turn for the worse since she'd had it carefully coiffed in preparation for the wedding. She was getting tired of the drab gray and was so looking forward to getting home to her beauty parlor and getting some color back. Her mind went briefly to Jeremiah and wondered how he felt about red hair. She'd have to sound him out, because she had a feeling that she'd be seeing him often in the future.

She gave a final rinse to her hair and pulled her mind back to the mysteries surrounding her. Why and by whom was Buzz killed? Was Amy's real estate agency involved? What drug was in Melanie's ring? Why was she killed? Why was Keisha abducted and left for dead?

Fonnie wrapped up in her fuzzy robe and stepped onto her balcony. She gazed out on what appeared to be the beginning of a beautiful day. The sun was dazzling, the surf was tranquil, the world smelled clean. She decided to walk the beach before breakfast. She called Brian's cell phone. He didn't answer, so she left a brief message. She pulled on a sweat suit and headed out.

She took deep breaths of the fresh, heady air, and sensed the coming of an early spring. She forgot for a few minutes that she was an old woman still not completely recovered from a stroke. In her mind, she was running barefoot over the sand, chasing the gulls, splashing in the waves. She was young, adventuresome, ready to take on the world.

A man's voice interrupted her fantasy. "Good morning, Fonnie. Want to take a boat ride?"

She turned to where the voice came from. Past the motel pier she saw Edgar Myers. He waved to her. She waved back. She walked a little faster and he strolled to meet her. "I don't see any boat," she said as she came closer.

"It's at the marina. I was headed that way. Felt like I had to get out, feel the ocean beneath me, breathe the salt air. Maybe say a decent good-bye to Buzz and Melanie. They both loved to go out for a fast ride." He took Fonnie by the arm and guided her around a large piece of driftwood. "Come and go with me. I could use some good company."

"Sounds tempting. I haven't been on a boat for over two years. But I can't. I have to get to the hospital and check on Keisha."

"How is she doing? Lula told me she still isn't remembering anything."

"That's right. The doctor says she may never remember what happened before or during the attack. It happens sometimes." Fonnie was surprised how smoothly the lie slipped through her lips. She didn't quite understand why she thought it necessary to lie, only that it had nearly become second nature and that she felt somehow she was protecting Keisha. "I guess it's just as well. Now she can go on with her life without a horrible memory hanging over her."

"I suppose so," Edgar said.

While they had been talking, they kept walking up the beach toward the marina. They were nearly at the dock when Fonnie looked back toward the motel. "I've got to be getting back and have breakfast. Then Brian can take me and Tyrone to the hospital. Tyrone must be anxious to get back."

Edgar pulled out his cell phone. "I'll call Brian and tell him not to wait for you. You're coming for a much needed boat ride. When we get back I'll treat you to breakfast and take you to the hospital."

"I don't know about that."

"Well, I do. Now what is Brian's number?"

Fonnie gazed longingly at the lapping waves, at the clear horizon. "Maybe just a short ride." She rattled off Brian's cell phone number. She'd always been good at remembering numbers. It was names that sometimes fell through the cracks.

Edgar punched in numbers and waited. "Brian, Edgar here. Your grandmother is with me. I'm going to take her for a short boat ride. You can go on to the hospital and I'll bring her later." There was a short pause, then Edgar went on, "Don't worry. I'll have her there in a couple of hours."

"A couple of hours? You said a short ride."

"Yes, but I have to feed you afterwards and I know for a fact you like a big breakfast."

"Someone has been telling on me." Fonnie headed to the marina pier. "All right, now which one of these monsters is your boat?"

"None. Mine is that small express cruiser bouncing around in the water like a rubber ball. Not that I couldn't afford a big one if I wanted, but I prefer speed over spaciousness. It's twenty-six feet of pure power."

Fonnie studied the sleek white boat with one bold red stripe along the side. She read the name, *Lula Baby.* "Your wife must be pleased that you named the boat after her."

"She hates it. In fact she hates boats in general. This boat has a cabin with all the necessities of life: galley, head, fridge, microwave, radio, and still she hates it. She especially hated all the time I spent on restoring this one."

"You restored it?"

"Sure did. It was a mess when I bought it. I scraped it down, practically redid the whole thing, repainted it. It was quite a job, but I loved it. Much more fun than buying a new one."

"I didn't realize you were such a hands-on person," Fonnie said. "Most attorneys I know prefer their desks to paint brushes."

"Not this one. I can hardly wait to get out of that office." Edgar led her to the side of the boat, stepped in and reached up a hand to help her aboard. His brawny, rough hand wrapped around her tiny frail one. "Easy now," he said. "Don't want you falling overboard." He pointed to a seat in the stern. "Sit there. You're in for the ride of a lifetime."

Fonnie sat, but her mind was on the previous conversation. "You planning on leaving the firm?"

He nodded. "As soon as I tie up some loose ends."

"Aren't you young to retire?"

"I have all I need to live on. I've managed to put aside a nice nest egg." He smiled and added, "in spite of having an expensive wife."

"Investments?"

"That's right. I've been lucky in my investments." Edgar carefully backed *Lula Baby* away from the pier. He steered the craft for open water and smiled at Fonnie. "Hang on. Here we go."

*Lula Baby* came to life like a dragon awakening from a nightmare. Fonnie was thrown sideways, her feet flew upward, her hands scrambled for something to hang on to. She yelled at Edgar, but her words were eaten by the wind. She found a handhold on the boat's railing and clung on like a terrified child. This was not the leisurely little boat ride she'd been expecting. What had been idle waves against the shore had turned into whitecaps, and Edgar was skipping over them at a right angle. The boat vaulted them effortlessly and then plummeted back into the water with a bone-shaking jar. Fonnie felt her teeth rattle and her butt bruise. She eyed the life jackets neatly fastened to the side of the boat just out of her reach. Why hadn't Edgar insisted she put one on before they started this wild ride?

At the other end of the boat, Fonnie saw Edgar

laughing at her. She loosened the grip of one hand long enough to shake a fist at him. Just wait until they got back to shore, she thought, he would hear some words that not even the most hardened sailor knew.

KEISHA WELCOMED her visitors with a wide smile. She'd been moved to a private room on the medical floor earlier, and the police officer had told her the ban on her visitors had been lifted. Even though she would still have a guard, she felt less like a prisoner. Tyrone came in first, gave her a giant hug. Jeremiah came up to the bed and squeezed her hand while Brian waved at her. She stared at the open door, saw the officer tilted back in a chair, nurses scurrying down the hallway. She turned back in disappointment. "Stephon?"

"I'm sorry, Sis," Tyrone said. "Stephon got a frantic call from his office and he had to go back. Said he'd call you later today."

"Of course," Keisha said. Her voice still sounded a little husky to her own ears, but the pain in her throat was gone. "His work must be piled up." She looked at the door again. "And Fonnie?"

"She'll be here later," Brian said. "She called earlier. Said she was going to take a walk on the beach. She wasn't back yet when we finished breakfast, so I left a note on her door that I was taking Tyrone to the hospital and would come back for her."

Tyrone shook his head. "It's a real affliction being without wheels. I could have been driving Keisha's car, but for some reason the police kept the keys."

"Really?" Keisha said. "I didn't know that. Surely they'll let you drive it home if I have to go by ambulance."

"They'd better. At any rate, I got Brian to drive me over. I wanted to give you Pop's latest message in person."

"And that would be?"

"That now you can talk, he wants you to call him yourself. He won't believe you're really all right until he hears it from you."

"Then I'll call him in a minute, and tell him the doctor is transferring me to the hospital there."

"That's great," Jeremiah said. "I guess that means we can all go home. I saw Clara and Tony and Midge off this morning. I suppose Hank and Doris will be leaving soon." He turned to Brian. "Do you know if the police have released Melanie's body yet?"

"I haven't talked to Steinberg this morning. I'll try to get up with him in a little bit."

"You do that while I go back and collect Fonnie." Jeremiah reached over and took Keisha's hand again. "You call your daddy now, and I'll be back with Fonnie soon."

Keisha leaned forward to wave good-bye to Brian and Jeremiah. As she did, her pillow slid out from behind her head, slipped down and got caught by the bedside rail.

Brian and Jeremiah left. Tyrone stretched over the bed, retrieved the pillow, and replaced it behind Keisha's head. He smoothed out the pillow, pulled up her bedcover and attempted to straighten the top of her nightgown.

As he touched her neck, Keisha gave a hoarse scream.

Brian, Jeremiah, and the police officer bolted into the room. Keisha was flailing her hands at Tyrone, pushing him back, trying to kick at him with her feet.

Jeremiah grabbed Tyrone by the arm, jerked him away from the bed. "She's having another flashback."

A nurse came running. With a soft voice and gentle touch, she tried to calm her patient. "It's all right, Keisha. No one is going to hurt you. I'm here with you. Everything is fine."

Keisha stared wildly at the group surrounding her bed. The nurse continued talking to her with reassuring words. "You're all right. Take some deep breaths now. Just relax. We're all your friends."

Keisha grasped the nurse's hand. "I'm sorry," she whispered.

"That's okay. You just had a bad memory. It's over now."

"No. It's not over," Keisha said. She shuddered as she pulled the sheet up higher. "I remembered. I know now who tried to kill me."

# THIRTY-ONE

FONNIE'S WILD RIDE continued until the shoreline became a blur and the buildings resembled a toy village. When she thought she couldn't hang on much longer, Edgar slowed the boat, and after a short while he cut the motor.

The boat bounced softy on gentle waves while Fonnie fought to regain her breath and her temper. She finally got them both under control. She smiled at Edgar. "No wonder Lula says she hates boats. I'm beginning to agree with her."

Edgar laughed. "I just wanted to show you how much speed this baby has."

"You did that. Now how about going back at a reasonable pace?"

"Sure," Edgar said, but he made no motion to restart the engine. "You know, sometimes I just like to come out here and be as one with the ocean, the sky, the breeze. Forget about everything that has happened back on shore. It makes all the hard work I put in on this boat worth while."

Fonnie gazed around at the peaceful scene. "Yes. I can understand that." But instead of making her forget about what had happened on shore, something he'd said catapulted a memory to the forefront of her brain.

It was about Hank and a crossword puzzle. Hank had asked her for a six letter word meaning *evidence of hard work*. She couldn't come up with one at the time, but now she knew the word. It was *callus*. Edgar had calluses on his hands from hard work—as did Tyrone. Only yesterday she'd given Tyrone a tube of hand cream to apply to his calluses and he'd made a remark about hard work.

Fonnie's mind skittered from calluses to Keisha's flashback. Tyrone had said that Keisha started fighting him when he touched her—touched her with his callused hands. Then Jeremiah had explained that Keisha wasn't fighting Tyrone but was trying to ward off her attacker. An attacker with the same kind of hands?

Fonnie shivered in spite of the sun's pleasant warmth. She studied Edgar's empty face as he gazed out at the horizon. There was no serenity, no agitation. Where, she wondered, was the man behind the face? Was this the face of a killer?

A cold fear quickened her pulse. Her breaths became faster and shorter. At the same time, she knew she had to keep her fear from being noticed. She did her best to keep her voice from quivering. "Guess its time to be getting back."

"Not yet. I think we need to talk a little."

"Talk? Here in the middle of the ocean?"

"What better place? No interruptions. No eaves-droppers."

Fonnie's trepidation kicked into high gear. Had the frenzied ride been a forerunner to a more serious danger? She tried to keep from panicking. "So what do you want to talk about?"

"Memory."

"Memory?"

"Yes. You told me Keisha couldn't remember anything about the night of her attack. And I understand that—lack of oxygen to the brain and all that good stuff. But I have a hard time believing that a woman with your remarkable mental agility can't remember a simple telephone conversation. Don't put on the innocent act with me. I want to know what Keisha told you that night."

So, Fonnie thought, her little trick to flush out the villain had worked, though not in the way she had envisioned. What to do now? She decided to go on the offensive. "You better take me back. Brian is expecting me, and he knows I'm with you."

"No. Brian isn't expecting you." Edgar gave a low laugh.

"But you called him," Fonnie said.

"I pretended to call him." Edgar laughed again. "Brian has no idea where you are. No one knows where you are."

Fonnie gave up all pretense of assumed calmness. "But they'll be looking for me."

"Oh, yes. Eventually, they'll start looking for you. And eventually they'll find you. Your body will wash ashore in a few days or weeks—perhaps miles from here. They'll wonder why you walked out into the surf or jumped off the pier or what freak accident landed you in the water. And I will be among your mourners, just as I'll be among the mourners for Buzz and Melanie."

"So you poisoned Buzz and strangled Melanie. Why?"

"It seems that you and I are much alike, Fonnie."

Before she could deny such a ridiculous statement, he went on. "We're both curious creatures. You want to know why Buzz and Melanie were killed, and I want to know what Keisha told you. Shall we trade information?"

From somewhere deep inside her, Fonnie found a little courage that hadn't yet evaporated. Edgar planned to kill her, but she wasn't dead yet, and she wasn't giving up. "As a matter of fact, I *would* like to trade info. You first."

Edgar leaned his head back and howled in laughter. "You're too much. I wish Lula had your sense of humor. But all joking aside, I'm holding the deck here and it's your first play."

Fonnie decided her best strategy would be to give him some real information. At this point, it couldn't hurt anything. "Keisha found a piece of paper in Buzz's pocket that indicated some monkey business at the law firm. She mentioned a couple of names, but the only one I recall is Klondike. She was going to turn it over to the police. She never got the chance. But since you have the paper now, you know what's on it."

"And you told the police about it?"

"Of course, I did. And they're getting a search warrant right now to go through every scrap of paper in your office."

"But they won't find a thing. I made sure of that."

"Then why are you so worried?"

"Not worried. Like I said, I was just curious."

"All right," Fonnie said. "Now it's your turn. Or should I guess? You killed Buzz because he was on to you, and you killed Melanie because she became suspicious. Right?"

"Not exactly. Actually it was Melanie who fed the drug to Buzz."

Fonnie gaped at him with unbelieving eyes. "Melanie? But why?"

"Because I paid her to do it—paid her a hell of a lot, I might add, to make it look like a natural death. It was no problem for her to get the medication at the hospital where she worked. And she knew just how much to give to make him sick and how much for a fatal dose. But when she insisted on more money, I kind of lost my patience. After her going away party, I went down to her room and suggested we take a walk to discuss it. She went willingly enough. We walked over to the chapel, and I took care of the situation."

Fonnie closed her eyes and tried to shut out the image of this horrible man with his hands around Melanie's throat. She didn't want to hear more, but she had to. "And Keisha?" she asked.

"I had gone through Buzz's things earlier trying to find any evidence he might have, but I came up empty. So when Midge called me about having Keisha clean out the room, I decided to keep an eye on her. As it happened, she left the door open a crack. I couldn't believe my good luck. She was so absorbed in her job that she didn't noticed me peeking in. I saw her take a piece of paper out of an inner jacket pocket. After she studied it a while, she became very upset. She shoved it into her pocket, quickly finished packing and carried the bags to her room. A short while later she ran down the stairs to the desk."

Edgar turned his gaze from Fonnie, back toward the

shore. A large boat seemed to be coming in their direction. Fonnie wondered if he would continue the story.

In a few moments his eyes again fixed on her. His voice changed to a bragging tone, as if he were proud of what happened next. "I saw Keisha take the stairwell down so I unscrewed the bulb and waited there for her to come back up. She struggled a little, but soon collapsed and I thought she was dead. I got the paper, but I didn't want to leave her there, so I d ragged her out the back door and carried her to the chapel to join Melanie. Fortunately, she didn't weigh much. It was a real bummer when I learned she'd come back to life. But since she doesn't remember anything, there's no harm done."

No harm done? What kind of monster was this man who sat across from her? And what was he going to do now that he'd spilled his guts?

Fonnie didn't have to wait long to find out.

# THIRTY-TWO

WHEN KEISHA CRIED OUT that she knew who had tried to kill her, it was as if a bolt of lightning had struck in the room. The nurse stepped backward so quickly she had to grab a chair to steady herself. The police officer immediately called Lieutenant Steinberg. Brian, Tyrone, and Jeremiah leaned over the bed waiting for her to go on.

Tyrone grasped her hand. "Are you sure?"

"I'm sure. I remember his hands. Steinberg said he wore gloves, but he didn't—not when he was choking me. He must have put the gloves on later." Keisha turned Tyrone's hand over and rubbed its surface. "He had calluses on his hands, just like Tyrone. It was Edgar Myers."

The officer relayed the name to the detective. "Sir, she says it was Myers." He listened for a moment. "Yes sir, I'll get the details while you start hunting him."

"I noticed his callused hands," Keisha continued, "when I was dancing with him at the reception. At the time, my mind compared them to Tyrone's. I was surprised because not many professional people have such work-worn hands."

Jeremiah had been nodding his head during the

recitation. "And that's why you had your flashback when Tyrone touched you."

"Yes, I felt those horrible hands around my neck again." She looked at Brian. "Couldn't the police have gotten his fingerprints from my neck? He certainly left enough of an impression."

"Occasionally forensics can get prints from flesh if it's done fairly soon," Brian said, "but if there's a delay, the oils in a person's skin will mess them up. In your case, it was over twenty-four hours and was too late. In fact, I'm sorry to say, your identification may not be enough. There are a lot of callused hands around."

The officer came up to the bed. "What he says is true, ma'am, but Lieutenant Steinberg is planning on taking him in custody on your say-so. Then we'll go from there."

"And I'm going back to the motel to tell Fonnie," Jeremiah said. "That woman is going to be one surprised cookie."

"I'm going too," Brian said. "Tyrone, you better stay with Keisha. We'll let you know as soon as there are more developments."

"Remember and tell me all that happens," Keisha called out in a weak voice as Brian and Jeremiah left. "I want to know everything the police do to catch that bastard."

"I promise," Brian called back. The two men exited the hospital together and each raced in his own car back to the motel. They joined up again on the elevator heading for Fonnie's room.

Brian stopped short when he saw the note he'd written still taped to her door. "She can't still be out walking. Where in the world do you think she is?"

"Probably enjoying the blueberry waffle special for breakfast," Jeremiah said. "Let's check the dining room."

They didn't find Fonnie in the dining room and the waitress said she hadn't been in. "I'd remembered if she had. She's not the type of person one forgets. I've waited on her several times this past week, but not this morning."

They didn't find Fonnie in the lobby or on the verandah. Brian scratched at his head. "I'm getting worried. Let's go check the pier."

STEINBERG'S FIRST STEP was to have his men swarm over the motel and its environs. Then he and an officer knocked on the door of Edgar's suite. After a delay, Lula came to the door. She answered his questions as well as she could. "No. I don't know where he is. I just got up. Edgar's an early riser. He may be with Hank, or he may have taken his boat out." She yawned, brushed hair out of her eyes. "What's this all about, anyway?"

"We need to ask him some questions. Where is his boat docked?"

"Pier one, slip three." She stifled a yawn and asked, "He's not in some kind of trouble, is he?"

Steinberg countered with a question of his own. "What makes you think he may be in trouble?"

"Nothing," Lula said. "I just want to know what's going on."

"I'll be back later and explain. Let me know if you hear from him."

As Steinberg and the officer with him moved down the hall, the officer asked, "Sir, shouldn't we have searched their apartment?"

"There's no reason for her to lie to us. She doesn't know we're on to him."

He radioed for some men to check the marina. The answer came back as Steinberg left the motel and headed down the beach. "His boat's gone, sir. And someone down here said they saw him leave. And get this, he had a woman with him—an old woman. What do you make of that?"

Steinberg looked up, saw Brian and Jeremiah coming toward him. "I hope it's not what I'm thinking." He closed the distance between himself and the two men in a few long strides. He got into Brian's face and bellowed, "Where's your grandmother?"

"That's what I'm trying to find out. No one seems to know."

"I think I know." He got on his radio again and requested a Coast Guard patrol boat and helicopter.

FONNIE HEARD the whirl of a helicopter's rotor blades in the distance. The sound seemed to be getting closer. If the copter came close enough, was there any way to send them a distress signal? And if she did, she wondered what Edgar would do. She tried to avoid looking up. Edgar was sitting idly at his end of the boat, his hands draped over the wheel. His glance would slide from her to the horizon and back again. What was he thinking?

The noise of the helicopter became louder. Edgar jerked his head up. "Damn!" He whipped his body around, started the engine.

The boat leapt forward. Fonnie flew backward. She grabbed the railing of the boat with one hand and waved frantically to the helicopter with the other. With each wave she sent a prayer heavenward: please let them see me, please let them help me, please let me get back home.

Edgar didn't seem to have any planned route. He swerved the boat back and forth, he turned around in circles, at one point he steered back toward shore only to make a U-turn and aim again out to sea. Fonnie was glad to see that the helicopter was staying right above them. Was it possible they had been searching for her?

Then her gaze fixed on another sight that brought her hope. A boat, running even faster than they were, was approaching from behind them. She didn't think Edgar was aware of it. He kept his eyes on the helicopter ahead and seemed intent on out-maneuvering it. He was smiling as he engaged in a game of cat and mouse, but in this case the mouse was teasing the cat.

All the time, though, Fonnie could tell that the boat coming from shore was gaining on them. She nearly broke out in a grin when she made out the letters C. G. followed by a number. The Coast Guard was coming to her rescue. She wondered how they had been alerted, but it didn't matter, someone was coming to help her. She forced herself to look away so she wouldn't alert Edgar.

ABOARD THE Coast Guard vessel, Brian, Jeremiah, Lieutenant Steinberg, and several officers and crewmen strained their eyes to see what was happening on the boat ahead of them. The man piloting the boat was clear enough, but the woman in the stern seemed to be crouched down. From time to time Brian would get a glimpse of gray hair flying in the wind.

The distance between the two boats was diminishing. "Hang in there, Gram," Brian whispered under his breath. "Help is on the way."

Brian noticed Jeremiah's hands were clenched onto the side of the patrol boat, his face ashen. Lieutenant Steinberg and the two officers with him had their guns drawn. Brian kept his eyes glued to his grandmother. He wondered why she never looked back.

AS THE COAST GUARD BOAT came nearer, Fonnie tried to calm herself with deep, even breaths. Her rescuers were closing in, and she wanted to be ready for whatever action she needed to take. She could tell the moment Edgar heard the extra motor in the background. He whirled around, saw the oncoming craft, pivoted back, and spun his boat at a quick right angle. The tactic took Fonnie by complete surprise. She lost her grip on the railing and her head fell backward.

In that moment Edgar sprang from his seat, reached Fonnie's side, and with one abrupt movement toppled her over into the swirling water.

# THIRTY-THREE

BRIAN SAW EXACTLY what happened. One second his grandmother was in the stern of the boat, and the next second she disappeared beneath the waves. Before he or any of the crew could react, Jeremiah kicked off his shoes and climbed up onto the side of the boat. One of the crewmen tried to pull him back. Jeremiah kicked loose and dove into the frigid ocean. The Lula Baby was hightailing it out of there, but the wake of the boat left a very visible path. Jeremiah swam toward where the boat had been.

Brian wanted more than anything else in the world to jump in beside him, but his common sense prevailed. He was a mediocre swimmer at best. If he jumped in, the crew would have an extra person to rescue.

The Coast Guard boat slowed and turned around. The chase would have to wait. The crew immediately started lowering life rafts. Steinberg and his men dropped their weapons and ran to help. Brian remained at the rail. He kept Jeremiah in sight while at the same time, trying desperately to see a bobbing head, a speck of gray hair, anything to show him that his grandmother was still alive. He saw nothing except the churning waves.

Jeremiah kept swimming toward where the boat

had last been seen. Brian tried to tell himself that if only Jeremiah could find Fonnie, he could keep her afloat until the life saving crew picked them up. But what if she hadn't survived the fall? Maybe that maniac Edgar had hit her with the boat when he took off. Or even now, she could be beginning to suffer from hypothermia.

Jeremiah swam with strong, sure strokes. Brian was astonished that the cold water didn't seem to bother him at all. The waves were becoming higher, perhaps because the rescue vessel was getting closer.

Jeremiah stopped swimming for a few moments and treaded water while his eyes scanned the area. Then he raised one hand in the air and motioned to his left. Brian's gaze followed the movement. To his amazement, he saw a head of gray hair coming toward Jeremiah. Gram was swimming! Her strokes were short and choppy, but she was making progress. Jeremiah hurried to meet her.

FONNIE LAY ON some kind of a bunk and shivered under layers of thermal blankets while Jeremiah sat on a stool wrapped in a blanket and held her hand. Brian gripped a mug of hot coffee and tried his best to get her to drink some. Fonnie was too tired and too cold to respond to them or to Lieutenant Steinberg's questions. She closed her eyes and tried to imagine a roaring fire on her hearth at home.

After what seemed like eons, warmth started to seep back into her bones. She leaned up on one elbow and smiled at Jeremiah. "I told you I used to be a good swimmer."

"You still are—an amazing swimmer." Jeremiah motioned for Brian to hand him the mug. "Now are you ready for some good hot coffee?"

She nodded. Her friend held her head up while she took several sips. "I just remembered," she said as her head dropped back down, "I haven't had breakfast yet."

Brian knelt down beside her. "When we get you warm and dry, I'm going to serve you breakfast in bed." He leaned over and kissed her on the cheek. "You had us pretty worried."

"You know, I was pretty worried myself. I didn't know I was taking a boat ride with a killer." She abruptly rose up on her elbows, looked frantically around the deck. "Where's Steinberg? Edgar's getting away. He has to go after Edgar."

Lieutenant Steinberg came up to her. "Not to worry, Mrs. Beachum. He won't get away. After we picked you up, I radioed the helicopter to keep him in view, and called for another Coast Guard vessel to pursue him. They'll have him in custody before long."

Fonnie stared at the detective. She liked Lieutenant Steinberg. She wanted to tell him everything she knew to help bring Edgar to justice. "He confessed to me. That is, he admitted killing Melanie, but he said Melanie killed Buzz."

Brian jerked back, his body stiffened, his voice cracked. "What? What did you say?"

Fonnie patted his arm. "I'm sorry, Brian, I shouldn't have blurted it out like that, but there's no easy way to tell it." Fonnie patted him arm. "Edgar paid Melanie to kill Buzz."

Steinberg spoke up. "That's about what we figured

out. Melanie's ring held the same drug that had killed Buzz. Being a nurse, she had easy access to it."

"Oh my God." Brian dropped his head onto Fonnie's blanket. "Oh, God, no."

Fonnie felt Brian shiver as he had done when he'd been a boy of nine and his dog, Toby, had gotten killed in the road. Melanie was not only dead, but everything he had felt for her was shattered. He struggled to his feet, his face contorted in grief. He closed his eyes, took a deep breath. "Give me a little time. I'll be all right." He walked over to a bench by the ship's rail, sank down and sobbed.

Steinberg reached over and pulled up a blanket that had slid off from Fonnie's shoulder. "Some of life's lessons come pretty hard. But he'll make it. I can tell he's got some of your grit."

"That's right. We'll all make it."

"You rest now," the detective said. "You've done your part to help solve the case."

Fonnie was glad to comply. She closed her eyes and slept the rest of the way back to shore.

An ambulance was waiting at the pier. Lieutenant Steinberg and Jeremiah both insisted Fonnie be checked out at the hospital. She knew it would be useless to argue. Jeremiah said he was going to take a hot shower and would see her later. "Brian and I will bring you some clean clothes to the hospital."

Fonnie searched Brian's haggard face. After he'd heard of Melanie's involvement in the crime, he hadn't said another word, and hadn't seemed to hear what others said to him. Grief etched his features, shadowed his eyes. As the boat neared shore, he came over, knelt down, kissed her on the cheek. He stood and stared over the side of the boat as if the waves could give him solace. Fonnie's heart broke for him, but she knew this was something he would have to weather in his own time, in his own way.

At the hospital, Fonnie was examined while Jeremiah updated Keisha and Tyrone about the morning's happenings. Brian joined the conversation when he told them of Jeremiah's heroic rescue. They assured Keisha that if Edgar had not yet been caught, he soon would be.

It was after two o'clock before Fonnie was resting comfortably in her motel room. She had foregone her promised breakfast in bed for ham and cheese biscuits at the local drive-in. They would do until she could get a decent dinner.

Amy and Paul's expected arrival had been pushed to the background during all the excitement. Now she was thrilled to think her daughter and new son-in-law would soon be here. Jeremiah was to pick them up at the airport at six fifteen. She was anxious for them to know all that had happened. She wanted to hear their take on Edgar's possible misdeeds that led to murder. But most of all she wanted Amy's reassuring and loving arms around her, to be reminded of how much family meant to her.

Fonnie put on a lovely lavender sweater, her dressy gray slacks, her strand of real pearls, and a little extra makeup. She knew Jeremiah would spend the time from the airport to the motel telling his passengers about murder and attempted murder. She intended to dispel any notion that she was an invalid recovering from a near-death experience.

THE REUNION, the conversation, the questions lasted late into the night. They went to a steakhouse for dinner, then to the hospital to see Keisha. Amy and Keisha greeted each other like long-lost sisters.

Paul was introduced to Tyrone and the boy responded with, "I'm delighted to meet you, Sir. Your reputation as an advocate for the underprivileged has come to my attention and I applaud your social conscience."

To which Paul replied, "Huh?"

Fonnie jumped in with an explanation. "I told him about you taking pro bono cases at the Women's Shelter."

"Oh, well, it's nothing." He smiled at Tyrone. "Fonnie has told me some pretty nifty things about you, too. She says you're a cinch to get a college scholarship."

"I'm working on it."

"Which means he has to get back to school," Keisha said. "Thank goodness the doctor has made all the arrangements for me to be transferred to Groverton tomorrow. Tyrone is going to drive my car home and then it's school for him while I work on my eating skills. I'm so wanting to get this IV out of my arm."

While they were at the hospital, Brian received a call from Lieutenant Steinberg. He managed a small smile as he hung up. "They've got Edgar. Since he wouldn't stop for the Coast Guard, they just waited until his boat ran out of gas."

Fonnie had mixed emotions. She was glad a murderer was in custody, but she was concerned about Lula. "Wonder what will happen to Lula."

Jeremiah shook his head. "I guess that depends on how much she knew—or suspected. She was a very unhappy lady. Maybe now we'll find out why she was unhappy."

Brian pivoted around to his mother. "And Mom, Steinberg wants to know if you and Paul can meet with him tonight. He's at the motel. Even before Edgar was apprehended, Steinberg had gotten a search warrant for the Myers' apartment and the motel offices. His men are going through everything now."

"Sure," Amy said, "but I don't know what I can tell him. And Paul didn't have any suspicions of Edgar."

"Maybe I should have," Paul said. "Maybe I should have made myself more available to Buzz. If Buzz had confided in me, this nightmare might have been avoided. I guess I was too wrapped up in my own happiness and didn't care about anything else."

Amy took his hand in hers. "You can't blame yourself for any of this. When you get back to your office, you can see if there are any clues to what Edgar was doing. In the meantime, we'll talk to the detective and answer all his questions."

They all said goodnight and good-bye to Keisha and made their way back to the now infamous Beachside Motel.

Brian called Lieutenant Steinberg and told him they would wait for him in the lobby. Fonnie was concerned about the detective when she saw his wearied face, his bloodshot eyes. "You need a good night's sleep," she said. "Now that the culprit is behind bars, can't you get some rest?"

He brushed back his tangled hair, scratched his head. "Soon. I just want to check one thing with Mr. and Mrs. Trent." He reached into an inside pocket and pulled out the piece of paper that Keisha had written for him. "We're looking for the original of this. Apparently, Mr. Garrison scribbled down some things that were going on at his office that bothered him. Miss Riggs found it, and later it was taken from her. Does it mean anything to either of you?"

Amy and Paul studied the paper. Finally Amy said, "The only notation I recognize is Trentstone Estates. I've sold some of those properties. It's an upscale development. But I don't know of any problem with it. Do you, Paul?"

"None of it makes sense to me. Could I have a copy of that? We're going home tomorrow and I can check in Buzz's and Edgar's offices. I might come up with something."

"That's your copy to keep. But I don't want you in your office until your local police have finished searching. I obtained a search warrant today, and they'll be going over everything. I'm sure you understand."

"Of course, I understand. You have to do your job. I hope you find what you're looking for."

"Me too. The police there will let you know if they remove any files."

Before Steinberg left, Fonnie asked him about Lula. "Is she all right?"

"She's cooperating. Says she doesn't know a thing about Edgar's business. She's spending the night in another room."

"But," Fonnie persisted, "is she all right? Is she horribly upset?" Fonnie paused. "Is she sober?"

"Yes, she's horribly upset. I think she loves her husband. But she's holding up well. And yes, she's sober."

"I won't have a chance to see her before we leave, but will you tell her I believe in her, and that I'll pray for her."

"Sure. I'll tell her."

IT WAS A somber group that said their farewells the next morning. There were hugs and handshakes all the way around. Tyrone took off first to follow Keisha's ambulance home. Amy and Paul left for home with Jeremiah close behind. Fonnie gave a big sigh as Brian pointed his car toward Groverton. "It'll be so good to be home again."

# THIRTY-FOUR

LIFE IN GROVERTON was soon back to normal. Keisha was released from the hospital after a few days and went back to her classes. Tyrone took his SAT and made great scores, especially on the verbal section. Brian was glad to get back to his own police district. And twice a week Fonnie caught the Senior Services bus to the "Y" to hone her swimming ability. One never knows, she thought, when it would come in handy.

Two gentlemen from Virginia also had the little town of Groverton, North Carolina on their minds. Stephon made frequent weekend visits, while Jeremiah kept the phone lines hot.

Amy and Paul's newly wedded bliss was snarled for a couple of weeks while investigators pieced together what Edgar had called his "investments." They drove down to tell Fonnie and Brian what they'd learned.

Fonnie could tell it bothered Paul to talk about the illegal activities of his senior partner, a man whom he had admired and respected. "It seems," Paul said, "that while Buzz and I were defending the underdogs against giant corporations, Edgar was feeding those same corporations material they could use in defense of their negligent or criminal actions. He was leaking to their lawyers ahead of time what type of evidence we had, giving them an opportunity to manufacture counter-evidence. They were paying him the big bucks that should have gone to our plaintiffs."

Brian listened attentively. "So Edgar was working against his own partners?"

"Not only us," Paul said, "but other trial lawyers as well. Here's where his networking really paid off. He played golf and partied with most of the other attorneys in town, as Buzz and I did. After I met Amy, though, I kind of dropped out of that scene. I preferred spending my time with her."

Fonnie noticed Amy moving a little closer to her new husband. They're a lovely couple, Fonnie thought for the thousandth time.

"As you know," Paul said, "Buzz was a hard worker, but he was also a real party animal. So he and Edgar spent a lot of time playing, drinking, and discussing cases with other attorneys. There was no actual disclosure of confidential information, but a smart person could figure out the particulars—and Edgar was smart. Then he sold those particulars to companies being sued.

"I don't know when Buzz started getting suspicious. He never said anything to me about it, but a few months ago he seemed worried about something. Our firm's income had dropped dramatically in the past year, and I thought perhaps he was troubled about finances, although we still were making adequate money. In retrospect, I think the Klondike case was the one that started Buzz investigating."

"I remember "Klondike" was one of the names on the paper Keisha found," Fonnie said. "Who was Klondike?"

"Klondike is a company that manufactures medical equipment. A man died from a defective pacemaker made by them. Buzz was prosecuting them on behalf of the widow. When the case went to court, their attorneys were able to rebuff every bit of his evidence. The widow received a token award rather than the millions due her. That must have set off alarm bells in Buzz's brain and he started looking back at other cases. He either said something to Edgar or Edgar realized what he was doing. I guess that's when Buzz's death warrant was signed."

Fonnie leaned forward in her chair. Something was being left out that made her uncomfortable. "But," she said, "what about Trentstone Estates? How did they come in?"

Amy answered the question. "That worried me too until I saw the original paper that Buzz had written. The police at Beacon Hill Beach found it hidden in his apartment at the motel and sent a copy to Paul. On it Buzz had written Trentstone, followed by question marks. Since Keisha had heard of the Trentstone Estates, she added the word "estates" when she duplicated the list. Actually, it had nothing to do with the development. Later Paul remembered a case involving a company whose CEO was named Trentstone. He looked it up and sure enough, the plaintiff lost that one too."

Brian had sat quietly through the recitation of facts, his face drawn, his eyes sad. When Amy paused, he asked Paul the question that must have been on his mind the whole while. "How did Melanie get involved?"

"The police told us that Lula knew Edgar and

Melanie were having an affair. Melanie used her visits to her Uncle Hank as an excuse to see Edgar, and many times when Edgar was supposed to be at Beacon Hill, he was actually in Miami. It seems that Melanie liked the high life, but her nurses' salary didn't quite cover it, so Edgar supplemented her income. Apparently when Edgar decided he had to get rid of Buzz, he called on Melanie for help. It was supposed to look like a natural death, which is why she made him sick before giving him the fatal dose."

"But she ran to his side to help him when he collapsed," Brian said. "We both did."

Fonnie's mind again pictured the two young people rushing to Buzz's side. Melanie seemed so competent as she evaluated her patient's condition, checked his pulse, made a mouth sweep with her finger to be sure his airway was clear. But what had she done just prior to that? Fonnie struggled to remember, then the picture came. The young nurse, bent over the stricken man, was fiddling with the ring on her left hand. Her right index finger scraped a substance from the ring before doing the mouth sweep. "Oh, God," Fonnie gasped. "The police said she had more of the drug in the ring. While pretending to help him, she gave him a final dose to be sure he wouldn't survive."

Brian looked like he was about to be sick. "And that's why Edgar insisted Melanie ride in the ambulance—to be sure Buzz didn't come to."

"And why Edgar opposed the autopsy," Fonnie added. "Melanie must have thought that since it was a small hospital, they wouldn't do a complete autopsy. I guess she learned that small doesn't mean sloppy."

Brian shook his head as if coming out of a bad dream. "So, Paul, where does that leave your law firm?"

"I'm bringing in a couple of bright, young fellows. We'll survive and do well again. And after Edgar's criminal trial, I plan to institute a civil one and go after his assets. That way, we may be able to compensate some of his victims."

"I know it's silly," Fonnie said, "but I can't help but worry about poor Lula. Where is all this going to leave her?"

"As a matter of fact," Amy said, "I had lunch with her last week. She sent her love to you, Mom. I should have mentioned her sooner, but all this other stuff got in the way."

"Never mind that. How is she coping?"

"Very well. Lula's a tough cookie. She's going to be penniless, but that's the way she wants it."

Fonnie scowled. "I don't understand."

"She's filing for divorce. Since she had signed a prenuptial agreement, even if Edgar ends up with any assets, she wouldn't get them. She wants to start over—and she wants to do it on her own."

"Good for her. But," Fonnie added, "what can she do? Did she ever hold a paying job?"

"Her last job was hostess in a night club. That's where Edgar met her. Now she has her sights on something a little different."

When Amy didn't say anything else, Fonnie exploded with, "What?"

"Real estate. She's going to take a realty course and get her license. And then…." Amy let her voice trail off.

Fonnie threw her hands in the air. "And then what? Come on, out with it."

"Then she's going to work for our agency. I think she'll make a great Realtor."

# EPILOGUE

FONNIE DRANK THE LAST of her breakfast coffee while lolling in her porch swing. She loved to get out of the house in the early morning, listen to the birds—some twittering, some warbling, and some just chattering. Brian had left for work and she was alone to enjoy her domain. Yesterday, Tyrone had mowed her yard, and now each blade of grass stood upright and proud covered with morning dew. The weather girl predicted another scorcher for today—typical for mid-July in the Carolinas, and it was already beginning to heat up. Fonnie took a deep breath, caught the scent of the honeysuckles growing up on the side of her house, and ambled indoors.

She sat down at her computer to check her e-mail. She had two messages. She read Amy's first. *Morning, Mom, We had Clara and Tony over for dinner last night. Clara is beginning to look like she swallowed a watermelon, and Tony keeps talking about the room they're redoing for the nursery. Paul is trying to decide if he wants to be called Grandpa or Paw Paw. I rather like Nana for myself. Love and kisses, Amy.*

The other message was from Jeremiah. After his sky-high telephone bill, he decided e-mail might be a better way to communicate. They wrote back and forth nearly every day—silly, inconsequential notes, but through them they had come to know each other very well. Then his weekend visit last month had really been delightful. He'd approved of her new hair color B*right* R*ose* R*ed*. They'd talked and laughed and smooched a little. They didn't try to define their relationship. Fonnie knew they would always remain good friends; if something else developed, that would be fine. She eagerly clicked onto his letter. *Greetings from God's Country, or Virginia, if you want to be more accurate. Just had a marvelous idea. How about us taking a trip together? Maybe spend a few days in Williamsburg? Visit with some of our ancestors? Think about it. Have a great day. J.*

Fonnie thought about it. A trip would be nice. Anywhere except to the beach. But first things first. She reread the invitation she'd received last week. She rubbed her fingers over the soft-textured vellum, traced the embossed names, *Keisha Louise Riggs* and *Stephon Dewey Weber*. What a lovely couple. Fonnie was so excited about the upcoming wedding, she almost felt like the mother of the bride again.